"I've dreamed of you..."

Ajax moved closer. Erin didn't step away, even though she knew she should, but right now she couldn't quite remember why. She was caught up in the intensity of Ajax's proximity and the way he was looking at her, and so when his head lowered toward her and his mouth touched hers, she felt nothing but a wild surge of desire.

Had he asked if he could kiss her? She didn't care. She'd given her assent just by accepting it. His mouth moved over hers, more insistent. Asking a question. Erin answered without hesitation, her mouth opening under his, allowing him to deepen the contact.

He moved closer, wound an arm around her back and pulled her into him where she could feel the hard thrust of his desire for her. It sent arrows of need right to her core, where she was melting and—

Ajax pulled his head back abruptly. "What's that sound?"

It took a second for Erin to register the cry of her baby. She reacted instantly, pushing free of Ajax's arms, and ran to the bedroom.

Irish author **Abby Green** ended a very glamorous career in film and TV—which really consisted of a lot of standing in the rain outside actors' trailers—to pursue her love of romance. After she'd bombarded Harlequin with manuscripts, they kindly accepted one, and an author was born. She lives in Dublin, Ireland, and loves any excuse for distraction. Visit abby-green.com or email abbygreenauthor@gmail.com.

Books by Abby Green

Harlequin Presents

Bound by Her Shocking Secret
A Ring for the Spaniard's Revenge
His Housekeeper's Twin Baby Confession

Hot Summer Nights with a Billionaire

The Flaw in His Red-Hot Revenge

Hot Winter Escapes

Claimed by the Crown Prince

Jet-Set Billionaires

Their One-Night Rio Reunion

Passionately Ever After...

The Kiss She Claimed from the Greek

Princess Brides for Royal Brothers

Mistaken as His Royal Bride

Visit the Author Profile page
at Harlequin.com for more titles.

Heir for His Empire

ABBY GREEN

HARLEQUIN
PRESENTS

HARLEQUIN®
PRESENTS™

Recycling programs for this product may not exist in your area.

ISBN-13: 978-1-335-59351-1

Heir for His Empire

Copyright © 2024 by Abby Green

For questions and comments about the quality of this book, please contact us at CustomerService@Harlequin.com.

TM and ® are trademarks of Harlequin Enterprises ULC.

Harlequin Enterprises ULC
22 Adelaide St. West, 41st Floor
Toronto, Ontario M5H 4E3, Canada
www.Harlequin.com

Printed in Lithuania

MIX
Paper | Supporting responsible forestry
FSC® C021394

Heir for His Empire

PROLOGUE

THE SEXUAL TENSION between Erin Murphy and the man in the elevator was thick enough to cut with a knife. A million and one sensations fizzed through her blood and body. Triumph. The satisfaction of a job well done. But more than all that was desire.

But even the word *desire* was too polite. It was sheer, raw lust. And danger. Illicitness.

Because the man was no mere man. He was her boss. Not even her boss. He was her boss's, boss's boss. With probably a couple more bosses in between.

It had been building for the last few weeks, while they'd been locked in rooms with the most intense negotiations taking place.

Obviously she'd been aware of how gorgeous he was. How sexy. The whole world knew it, and it had hit her right between the eyes the day she'd been hired on to his legal team as an attorney, proving she was no different from the masses. But she'd buried it down deep—because she knew it was *so* inappropriate to fancy him, and because she was eager to make a good impression. This was her first job since completing a master's degree in corporate law, and she'd been hired specifically because of that additional expertise.

She'd thought she'd had her crush under control. Until these last few weeks of being in the professional equivalent of a pressure cooker.

Ajax Nikolau was a Greek god. Or, as near to a god as a mortal could be. Beautiful, with mesmeric deep-set green-blue eyes that popped from a chiseled face, and a mouth that called to mind sin and sex. Thick wavy dark hair. Tall, powerful build. Athletic. He wore suits, but the way they moulded to his sculpted form was downright provocative.

Together with a mind as sharp as a rapier, it was a potent combination.

He was also, arguably, one of the wealthiest men in the world—since approximately an hour ago, when the last contract had been signed. He now had full control of his family logistics business. He'd been rich before—astronomically—but now he was on a par with fabled Indian steel magnates and media titans.

But Erin didn't care about any of that. Because it didn't mean anything to her beyond the fact that she'd done her job. All she could see was *him*. The man. Flesh and blood. Sinew and bone. Hard muscle. Eyes blazing with a heat that connected directly to her core in a way that had never happened to her before.

They'd had champagne to celebrate with the rest of the team after the signing, and the sparkling wine still lingered in her veins like bubbling electricity. She couldn't believe that this was happening. Even though nothing had actually been articulated. It was in the air. Potent.

Just moments ago they'd been in the foyer of Ajax Nikolau's office building in downtown Manhattan, and as Erin had been about to leave, along with the rest of the legal team, he'd called her name.

She'd turned around, fixing a polite smile to her face. 'Yes?'

'I have some papers in my home office. I think it's best if you take them for safekeeping. Is that okay?'

Erin had frowned briefly. The last thing Ajax Nikolau had to worry about was the security of anything. The man was more well-guarded than a head of state. Along with his offices, he had properties strewn from one end of the globe to the other. So it had been an odd request.

But then she'd looked into his eyes and she'd seen the veneer of civility stripped away.

He wants me.

It had hit her like a thunderbolt right in the gut. She'd suspected, but whenever she'd caught him watching her over the previous weeks she'd looked away, telling herself she was being ridiculous. Mortified to have been caught looking at him.

Why on earth would a man like Ajax Nikolau be remotely interested in a woman like her? She didn't incite men to paroxsyms of desire. Especially not men like him. She was reasonably fit. Her features were symmetrical enough. But there was nothing about her that drew attention, and that was how she liked it.

Except now she was in this elevator, with *him*, and she had to face the unbelievable fact that somehow she'd drawn the eye of one of the most exciting men in the world. There wasn't enough oxygen going to her brain for her to try and figure out why.

This was, without a doubt, the most spontaneous, out-of-character thing she'd ever done in her life.

Meanwhile the elevator kept ascending to the penthouse. And suddenly Erin went cold with a flash of panic. What if she'd read the signals wrong? What if the triumph of the deal, the champagne, had all gone to her head and here she was, mentally climbing the man like a monkey, when he literally meant to just give her some papers and send her on her way?

But then, as if reading her mind, he put out a hand, pressed a button, and the elevator came to an incongruously smooth stop between floors.

Nikolau's voice was a little rough. 'Just so we're clear: I want you, Erin. But you're under no obligation to do anything except take the papers and leave.'

Erin gulped. *Had* he read her mind? Had she spoken out loud?

He does want me. I'm not hallucinating.

A mixture of relief and dizzying excitement made her tremble. She said faintly, 'There are actually papers?'

He nodded. 'But I won't lie. I used them as a pretext to get you alone. For weeks now you've been driving me crazy. I know this is crossing a million boundaries—and, believe me, if I felt I could resist... I would.'

His jaw clenched at that, as if he was irritated with himself, with his own lack of control.

The mere thought of pushing this man to the edge of his control was beyond heady.

Something ridiculous occurred to her. 'What do I call you?' She'd always referred to him as 'Mr Nikolau', even though he had said to them all that they should call him Ajax.

'My name is Ajax.'

She tried it out. 'Ajax...' It felt strange. Illicit.

He touched her jaw. 'I like the way it sounds when you say it.'

Erin might have rolled her eyes if she'd been less in awe and not still reeling.

What he'd just said—that he couldn't resist her—was just so beyond her comprehension of who she was—essentially boring—that she almost felt like giggling a little hysterically. But then the look on his face stopped her. It was stark. Hungry.

For her.

Plain, academic, serious Erin Murphy.

She'd led an academically driven existence for as long as she could remember. As the only child of a professor, it was all she'd really known. Her life had rarely, if ever, been given over to moments of spontaneity or just…fun. Not that this moment could be described as 'fun', exactly, when Ajax was looking at her with such an intense expression that she realised she'd never really seen him smile.

She knew there were reasons for that—he'd tragically lost his wife and child in an accident some years ago—and suddenly, as if galvanised by that reminder, and the sense of her own somewhat staid life, instead of doing the sane thing, the *safe* thing—stepping back out of this moment of madness—Erin moved towards him. Towards the madness.

She touched her mouth to his, trembling all over. For a second he didn't move, and Erin became acutely aware that she was pressed up against a wall of steel. She went cold again. Maybe she'd overstepped the mark? Even though he'd told her he wanted her, maybe he was the kind of guy who didn't appreciate women making the first move?

But before she could overthink it he took her elbows in his hands, holding her to him, and his mouth moved over hers. Any suspicion that she'd done the wrong thing because she'd initiated contact was gone. Melted. Turned to ash.

She couldn't feel her legs. His mouth was hard and soft, demanding but asking, all at once. It was like no kiss she'd ever experienced. Erin had to pull back for a second, dragging in a breath. Her vision was blurred. Kissing Ajax was like being pulled into a vortex, going faster and faster.

As if he sensed she was overwhelmed, he stopped and cupped her jaw. She felt her hair being freed from its tidy chignon, falling around her shoulders. His eyes followed the movement, and then his fingers were in her hair.

'It's like burnt gold.'

She couldn't find a breath. He was making her hair sound…extraordinary. But really it was nothing special. It wasn't blonde, or red…it was somewhere in between. Her mother's hair. But her mother was the last person Erin wanted to think about at that moment, because thinking of her inevitably brought painful memories of abandonment, so she reached for his tie and loosened it, opening his top button of his shirt.

The hollow at the bottom of his throat was exposed, and it felt ridiculously intimate even though they were both still fully clothed.

As if reading Erin's mind again, Ajax pushed her jacket off her shoulders and it fell to the ground. Long fingers efficiently undid the silk bow at her neck and then moved down to her buttons. She imagined them slipping free of the silk, eager to please him.

She almost felt like giggling again, but sobered up when he pushed her open shirt aside and looked at her for a long moment. At her breasts, encased in silk. Erin felt a blush rise into her face. She'd always had a slightly embarrassing preference for expensive materials close to her skin. A taste for luxury that didn't exist anywhere else in her life.

He dislodged her shirt so that it fell off one shoulder. He slipped his fingers under the strap of her bra, dropping it onto her arm, and the cup immediately fell down over the curve of her breast.

She shivered.

Erin had no idea what to expect…she hadn't gone as far as audaciously fantasising about what it would be like with a man like this. But she knew she never would have imagined this…this exquisite slow-burn torture.

He cupped her breast and her nipple pinched tight. Her breath became more shallow. And then he lowered his head and his mouth closed over the straining tip.

It was like an electric shock to the system, the laving of his tongue and the sucking of his mouth…all that hot moisture. Her hands tangled in his hair. She couldn't even remember putting her hands there. She wanted to do the same to him—take off his clothes, bare him—but he was kissing her again and palming her breast, fingers trapping that nipple and pinching.

She gasped into his mouth.

His tongue was hot, demanding, and she had no choice but to submit with an eagerness that might have mortified her if she'd been capable of rational thought.

Erin could feel his erection pressing against her and she moved against him instinctively, seeking more contact. He pulled her skirt up, bunching it over her hips, and then his fingers were spreading over her thigh, lifting it to hook her leg around his waist, bringing her into even deeper contact with his body.

She broke the kiss. His hardness was *right there*. At the apex of her legs. Where every nerve-ending was throbbing.

Erin wanted to free him and push her underwear aside, so there would be no barrier to a more intimate connection. The need was so intense she could hardly breathe.

She tried to communicate it with her eyes. She'd never wanted anything so badly. So urgently. *Here. Now.*

Time stood still, and for an infinitesimal moment she could see that he was as hungry as her. But then something flickered across his face. So fast she couldn't decipher it. Yet it looked like shock.

He pulled back, and Erin almost whimpered. Mortifyingly.

He put her leg back down and said roughly, 'Not here... like this. I'm sorry. I don't know what came over me.'

Erin's brain was too heated to fully understand until he pushed the elevator button and it softly jolted into movement again. Upwards. She breathed out when she realised he wasn't taking them back down to the ground level.

They ascended so high her ears popped. Then the elevator stopped again and the doors opened, straight into what had to be Ajax's apartment. She'd never been there. His offices were a few levels down.

The apartment was sleek and minimalistic. Huge ceiling-to-floor glass windows. Modern art on the walls. Sofas and chairs that looked inviting but which Erin had a feeling had never really been sat in. She knew Ajax tended to entertain in venues. Not at home.

Even though she'd been working for him for weeks, she still wasn't used to the level of opulence in his world. But she wasn't given a chance to linger or look around. He took her hand and led her silently through the dimly lit space, down a corridor and into a room at the other end of the apartment.

His bedroom. There were huge walls of glass again, giving what had to be a breathtaking view of lower Manhattan at night, a glittering skyline of lights. The blinking lights of a helicopter flew across the night sky.

But then it was all eclipsed. Because Ajax turned her around to face him and she swallowed. Suddenly intimidated to be here, in his private space.

'Are you sure you want to do this, Erin? You can stop… walk away at any time.'

Something inside her eased. She'd known he was a man of integrity after watching him do business, but to have him really care about her consent was something she hadn't even realised she needed.

She nodded. 'I want this.' *You.*

She'd never considered herself a very sexual person. She'd had one boyfriend in college, here in Manhattan, and they'd both decided to amicably split up when they'd graduated and he'd moved to Los Angeles. There had been no major grief. She'd had no intention of leaving New York, where she'd been born and had grown up. And the sex… Her boyfriend was the only person she'd had sex with, and at no point had she ever felt for him what she was feeling now.

Desperate. Hungry.

It was exhilarating and terrifying all at once. As if she wasn't as in control of her own reactions as she'd always thought she was. Erin was a cerebral person, and she'd never been so aware of her body.

Ajax started to take off his clothes. Jacket shucked off and thrown to the floor. Tie pulled off. Shirt opened, revealing a broad, muscled chest with a dusting of hair across his pectorals.

Erin had hardly caught her breath when his hands were on his trousers and he was undoing them, pushing them down over lean hips. Stepping out of them. Shoes and socks gone.

Now he stood before her fully naked, and she was…in shock. She didn't know where to look and she wanted to look everywhere. Her gaze travelled over inches of dark golden flesh, the evidence of his lineage from Greece. Down further. Flat stomach, slim hips and…his erection. She gulped. He was big. The sheer evidence of his virility was daunting.

'I'm feeling a little underdressed here, Erin.'

She looked up and could see his mouth twitching. That beautfiul sexy mouth.

Her heart hitched. *Oh, my.*

She realised her own state of undress. Shirt and bra half on, half off. Jacket gone. Still in the elevator? Skirt still ruched up over one thigh. Hair tumbling over her shoulders. Too long. She hadn't had time to get it cut.

Before she could figure out where to start, Ajax stepped close and pushed her shirt down over her arms and off. It fell to the floor. He reached around behind her to undo her bra. It too fell away.

For some inexplicable reason Erin didn't feel self-conscious. Maybe it was because Ajax had already bared himself. He reached for the fastening at the side of her skirt and opened it, easing it down over her hips.

Now all she wore was the matching underwear. Silk and lace. Decadent.

Ajax looked down. 'I like your choice in underwear.'

'Thank you.'

Literally words she'd never have expected to be exchanged between them, when up to this evening any dialogue had been focused solely on the dense legalese of delicate contract negotiations.

'May I?'

She wasn't sure what he was asking until he was at her feet, looking up. Another revelation. Ajax Nikolau at her feet. She nodded dumbly.

He tugged the sides of her panties down over her hips and thighs until they were at her feet. She stepped out of them.

But Ajax didn't stand up. He said, 'Sit on the edge of the bed.'

Erin realised it was right behind her. She fell more than sat on the edge. Ajax put his hands on her knees, pushing them apart. Her heart was thumping so hard she thought it must be audible, but his gaze was fixed on her body, giving her an awareness of sensuality she'd never experienced before.

He stroked the back of his hand over her belly. Her muscles quivered.

'Your skin is so pale...'

Erin felt breathless. 'My parents were...are Irish... Or at least...you know...second or third generation.'

Ajax looked at her, a glint in his eye. 'With a name like Murphy I never would have guessed.'

Her mouth almost fell open. He was joking with her! But now he was looking at her body again, moving between her legs, forcing them further apart. Cupping her breasts.

'I used to fantasise about this during all those boring moments in the negotiations. You became a distraction.'

Erin struggled to get the words out, 'You fantasised about...this...?'

He nodded. His thumbs were moving back and forth over her nipples and it was hard to focus on what he was saying—which was annoying, because what he was saying was...unbelievable.

'I fantasised about what was under your prim suits. The silk shirts, the tight skirts… Do you have any idea how delectable your ass looked in those skirts?'

She shook her head. And then a memory flashed back. She'd been helping herself to some coffee during a break recently, and had bent down to pick up a fallen spoon. When she'd turned around she'd almost dropped her coffee cup. Ajax had been staring at her so broodingly she'd thought she'd done something wrong.

He leant forward now and placed his mouth over one nipple, sucking and then biting gently. Every cell in Erin's body seemed to spasm at once with pleasure. Ajax put his hands around her back, holding her to him as he administered the same torture to the other breast, until they were throbbing peaks of exquisite pain/pleasure.

And then he pulled away. 'Lie back.'

She did, almost relieved at the respite. But there was to be no respite.

He pushed her thighs apart and she felt his eyes on her. Then his breath feathered on her inner thigh, his lips glancing across her skin as he came closer and closer to where all her nerve-endings were tingling… His breath was hot, but not as hot as his mouth when he pressed his lips and tongue to the core of her body.

Erin had to bite down on her hand to stop screaming, even though she was pretty sure there was no one to hear them. The man was remorseless, exploring her with a thoroughness that made her whole body clench, as if she could possibly stave off the inevitable.

She couldn't. It broke over her in an unstoppable wave. She had nowhere to hide. She'd never been so exposed, and yet she'd never felt more liberated. With her boyfriend, sex had felt self-conscious and a little laborious. Her orgasms hadn't had the power to break her apart. Sex had never felt this earthy or raw.

She was barely aware of Ajax moving, doing something, before he moved her up the bed as effortlessly as if she was a boneless, pliant lump of flesh.

He was on his knees between her spread legs and she looked up to see him rolling protection onto his body. His very hard body... Erin's inner muscles clenched in response.

He looked at her. 'Are you okay?'

Was she? There wasn't a word invented for what she was right now. All she could do was nod. Stupidly.

He put his hands on her thighs and lifted her up towards him so that his erection was nudging the slick folds of her body.

But then he stopped and looked at her. 'You're not... innocent?'

Erin shook her head quickly, a little mortified by how desperate she was to feel him inside her. Her voice was rough, breathy. 'No...but it's been a while.'

'We'll take it slow.'

Erin silently begged for mercy, because she knew this was going to be— *Ohhhh!* He thrust into her in one fluid, cataclysmic movement, watching her reaction. Her back arched. He was so big... She felt stretched, just on the border of being uncomfortable, but then he went deeper and she let out a shaky breath.

She'd never felt so...full.

Ajax adjusted his body so that he was almost completely over her. He slowly withdrew and she could feel her muscles massaging his length. His jaw was gritted. Sweat sheened his brow. Erin's own skin was slick with perspiration.

He moved back in again, and she gasped at the sensation as little flutters of pleasure emanated from the centre of her body. He moved rhythmically, in and out, and her tension wound higher with each move of his body.

Desperation pooled low inside her... An urgency. A need for *more*. She wasn't even aware she'd spoken out loud until Ajax was moving faster, going deeper.

Harder.

Had she said that? But soon he was moving with more force and her head tipped back. There was a force building inside her and she wanted to plead or beg, but she couldn't articulate what she needed.

Ajax threaded his fingers through hers and held her hands above her head. She felt like growling at him. She bit his shoulder. She heard a low huff of a chuckle.

I made him laugh.

But before that could register, he was releasing her hand and cupping her breast, feeding it to his mouth, teeth nipping at her sensitised flesh. Suddenly everything went very still—and then she was falling, tripping, end over end, down into a whirlpool of pleasure so intense that this time she couldn't stop herself from crying out.

She was only barely aware of Ajax's guttural shout as he followed her, his big, powerful body slumping over hers. She put her arms around him without even realising what she was doing.

A month later

Ajax stood at the window. Fully dressed. As if his clothes were some kind of armour.

Against what? asked a snide voice.

Against the naked woman behind him on the bed.

She was still asleep. He could see her reflection in the

window. The pale skin, the graceful curves. The soft swells of breasts and buttocks and the flare of hips.

The long red-gold hair spread over the pillow. The same hair that trailed across his chest and down as she explored his body with her mouth, before wrapping a hand around him and—

Skata! Enough.

She was just a woman. Like any other.

So why had he vowed not to touch her again after that first night?

Because he'd known, even then, that what they'd shared had been...unprecedented, and that it should not be indulged again because he was not looking for encounters that went beyond being casual.

He'd woken the following morning—late. Unheard of for Ajax, who hadn't slept past dawn for years. He'd felt hungover. As if he'd been drinking. But it hadn't been a hangover from drink—again, not usual for him. It had been a sex hangover.

He'd had his share of sexual experiences—he wasn't a monk—but he'd never had sex like that. He'd had to have her. It had been building for weeks. She'd been distracting him from work. Unheard of.

In the aftermath of that night he'd put their chemistry down to the intense circumstances leading up to the negotiations that had finally put him in full control of Nikolau Industries.

Ajax and his legal team had been all but sequestered for weeks, in order to prevent any leaks. So it was no wonder he'd started to notice Erin Murphy, the newest member of his legal team. Who, he'd been assured upon her appointment, was brilliant.

She hadn't said much at first. Just watched. And listened.

She'd been quiet. But something about her had kept drawing his eye. Something about her poise. Her quiet confidence. While others jockeyed for attention or kudos, she didn't.

Then one day, when tensions were high, there'd been a dispute about the wording of part of the contract. In the heated tense silence between arguments she'd posited a totally novel way to word it that had instantly defused the situation.

Ajax had seen in that moment that she'd made a couple of enemies among the more ambitious of the group, but she'd seemed oblivious.

She'd intrigued him in a way that no one else ever had. He'd found himself looking for her every day. Checking she was there. One day she hadn't been there, and her boss had informed Ajax that she was working on another project.

Ajax had told him to bring her back, as he didn't want the contract team broken up before they'd reached agreement. Which hadn't been entirely untrue. But his main motivation had been purely selfish.

The following day she'd been back in the room and their eyes had met. That was the other thing that had intrigued Ajax. She hadn't looked away. Not for a long moment. She hadn't been fazed by his regard. She hadn't sensed his interest and then exploited it, as most women would.

The sense of intrigue had grown into full-blown lust. Until it had been hard to focus or think straight. She wore practically the same thing every day. Pencil skirts. Silk blouses. Jackets. Court shoes. Muted colours. Minimal make-up and jewellery.

But she was provocative. Ajax hadn't been able to put his finger on why and that had irritated the hell out of him. He'd become transfixed by wondering what she would look like if her hair was down. And what was underneath those suits? Was she pale all over?

Her hair was a unique shade of dark strawberry blonde. He'd found himself wondering if she had hair the same colour *there*, guarding her sex, and that had resulted in a raging erection. In the middle of a meeting. Humiliating.

By the time the deal had been done and they'd celebrated there'd been no way he wasn't going to explore his fascination. He hadn't even been sure if she wanted him too—but as soon as he'd asked her to wait and she'd looked at him with those huge hazel-brown eyes, colour scoring her cheeks a tantalising blush, he'd known that she did want him.

They'd barely lasted a few seconds in the elevator. It had been the hottest, most erotic experience of his life.

But the following morning, when Ajax had woken late, she'd been gone. Long gone. He'd never experienced that before. Most of his lovers were all too keen to cultivate intimacy the next day—which was why he never hosted lovers in his own home. Something he'd apparently forgotten that night.

She hadn't even left a note. And when Ajax had seen her in the office a few days later, she'd looked at him as if nothing had happened. On one level he'd known he should be welcoming her lack of clinginess, but on another level he'd been incensed.

Had she not enjoyed the night? It had blown his mind... That suspicion alone—that she hadn't experienced it the way he had—had made him feel exposed and uncomfortable.

Eventually he'd managed to get her alone and he'd asked her what was going on.

'What do you mean?' she'd asked.

'We slept together, Erin.'

'Yes, I know.'

'You left the following morning.'

She'd gone a little pink at that reminder. 'I didn't think you'd appreciate waking up to find me making breakfast.'

The fact that she was right hadn't comforted Ajax. Perversely. And then he'd realised what was going on. He'd cursed himself.

'This is a play, isn't it?'

She'd frowned. 'What do you mean?'

'You're playing coy because you know it'll engage my interest and curiosity.'

She'd looked angry—the first time he'd seen any extreme of emotion on her face. And the fact that he'd noticed had made him feel more prickly.

She'd said tersely, 'I don't play those kinds of games. I thought I was doing us both a favour…that neither of us wanted a post-mortem. It was just a one-night thing.'

Ajax had been a little speechless. He'd realised he believed her. And that she was speaking sense. Women didn't usually captivate him to the point where he had to discuss anything.

Feeling exposed, he'd said, 'You're right.'

And so he'd walked away. And brooded for almost a month. But every time he'd seen her she'd seemed utterly serene—as if their night wasn't lingering in her blood and body the way it was in his, no matter how much he tried to deny it. Like a decadent aftertaste of something that you just want one more bite of.

Just a one-night thing…

But what about one more night?

It became an obsession. If he had one more night with her surely it would burn out—whatever this fascination was?

And so he'd said it. Yesterday. After a meeting he'd asked her to stay behind and he'd asked her bluntly, 'Do you want one more night?'

She'd looked at him, cheeks going pink. Suddenly the veneer of serenity was slipping and Ajax had felt something victorious move through him.

She still wanted him.

'I...' She'd hesitated. 'I'm not sure if it's a good idea.'

'I think it's the only way we can move on.'

It was definitely the only way he could move on.

'You think one night is all it'll take?' she'd asked.

No. But he ignored the assertion. That was the lust talking. No woman had ever held his interest for longer than one or two nights.

He'd nodded. 'Absolutely.'

There had been a long moment, as if she was battling some inner demon, but then she'd said, 'Okay. When and where?'

Ajax liked that about her. Straight up. As she'd said, she didn't play games. And so she'd come up to his apartment last night.

Ajax had planned on them having dinner, but as soon as the elevator doors had closed behind her any attempt to be civilised had disintegrated. They'd been naked in seconds.

They hadn't eaten dinner until midnight—a surprisingly companionable interlude, with Erin dressed in one of his shirts, sitting on opposite sides of the kitchen island, picking at chicken salad and drinking wine.

It had been so unlike anything he'd ever indulged in with a woman he'd found it disconcerting. It had reminded him uncomfortably of the past, and how different it had been with his wife—a woman he'd committed to in the most permanent sense, in spite of the fact that he'd had no feelings for her.

Yet suddenly Ajax had found himself comparing the two experiences and wondering what it might be like to actually like a woman enough to want to spend more time with her...have a relationship.

A sound came from behind Ajax on the bed. He tensed against the inevitable surge of blood. Of awareness. So much for hoping one more night would douse the fire... He feared it had only made it worse. Even more reason, though, to do what he had to now. To say what he had to.

Because one thing was certain after last night: this woman was a danger to him. To everything he believed and had built up.

He wasn't in the market for a relationship and never had been. It wasn't in his DNA and never would be. Not after what had happened. If there ever had been a moment when he might have been persuaded, it had died a long time ago.

He steeled himself and turned around. Erin was up on one elbow, looking deliciously sleepy and well-loved. She had pulled the sheet up to her chest. Ajax lamented it while at the same time welcoming it. He didn't need the distraction. She'd distracted him enough.

'Morning,' she said, and her voice was husky enough to almost make him change his mind. *Almost.*

But he was stronger than that. He had to be. He had a duty to his business and he had to transcend personal temptations.

Ajax had had his chance to make a personal life work and it had ended in tragedy. There would be no more *personal* for him, and it had been a mistake to allow Erin Murphy under his guard again.

If anything, last night just proved that he should have

listened to his gut the first time round. The fact that the woman was making him even think of personal temptations and reminding him of what he'd lost was all the proof he needed. She was exposing his weakness and he could not afford to be weak.

Ajax said, 'We need to talk.'

CHAPTER ONE

Twenty-one months later, Manhattan

ERIN STOOD BY the cot, watching her one-year-old daughter finally—mercifully—fall into sleep, legs and arms splayed as if fighting to the very end. The small room was bathed in dim undulating lights that threw various shapes of unicorns, dogs, rabbits and birds across the ceiling, chasing each other on a loop.

Erin smiled as she looked at her. She was a sturdy, feisty little thing and she didn't resemble Erin at all. She was all her father. Dark skin...dark curly hair. The only thing she'd taken from Erin were her hazel eyes.

Erin had almost grown used to the ache near her heart whenever she looked at her and was reminded of Ajax Nikolau—which was far too often for comfort. The ache was fast turning into a kind of heartburn.

Her conscience pricked. *Hard.* Her father had been minding Ashling today and he'd said it to her again.

'You can't keep putting it off. He needs to know. She's almost walking.'

Erin knew he was right. She'd made attempts to let Ajax know—she'd even written him a letter—but there had been no response and she'd not pushed it, partly because it had been a reminder of his rejection, but also because of unwelcome memories from far closer to home, within her own family.

She'd told herself she had more important things to get on with. Namely becoming a single parent to her daughter and searching for a new job.

In fairness, Ajax had pointed out that she wasn't under any pressure to leave, and that if she'd requested a transfer to a different office or department they wouldn't have to see each other again. She could stay working for the law firm his company used—it was vast.

She'd been tempted. It would have made things easier. But even without having to see him she knew that she would have been aware of him. And people talked. He was a dynamic, enigmatic man. Single. Available. She would have heard gossip about who he was with. And, as much as Erin would have liked to deny it to herself, and pretend that what had happened between them was just physical, he'd crept under her skin and got to her on an emotional level.

Which she knew was ridiculous. They'd had one conversation outside of the bedroom, that second night, and needless to say that hadn't strayed into anything personal.

Erin had known she was way out of Ajax Nikolau's league—that what had happened between them had been as out of character for him as it had been for her. That was why he'd dumped her so unceremoniously after that second night.

Erin's break-up with her college sweetheart hadn't sliced as deep as that rejection by Ajax. Even before the unanswered letter, it had called to mind the deep and abiding pain of her mother's rejection and abandonment, and its effect on her father, when Erin had been just a toddler. A pain that she had successfully managed to avoid all her life by not allowing anyone to get too close.

But Ajax had got too close. And that had terrified her. So she'd accepted his ending of their brief affair.

When she'd been head-hunted by a rival firm not long afterwards, she'd used the opportunity to leave. They'd been good to her, considering her pregnancy, and she'd been working part-time for them since returning from maternity leave recently.

So, to say things had changed drastically since her short-lived affair with Ajax Nikolau was putting it mildly.

Erin grimaced and moved silently out of the baby's room, half closing the door behind her.

Frankly, she was too exhausted to think about any of that now. She finally had a moment to heat up her dinner and—

The buzzing of her doorbell broke through Erin's thoughts. She assumed it was a mistaken delivery—drivers often pressed the wrong apartment number—but when she lifted the receiver and the camera came on she went cold all over.

It wasn't a delivery driver. It was a man. Too tall for his face to be visible on screen. All she could see were wide shoulders and a suit, but even through the grainy image she could appreciate the cut of the suit and the distinctive breadth of the chest and shoulders.

And then a face came into vision—devastatingly gorgeous, instantly recognisable. *Ajax Nikolau.* The fact that he was here, just a few floors down, as if manifested straight out of her guilty imagination, was unbelievable. So unbelievable that Erin found herself pushing the button to admit him before she'd even made the decision to let him in.

She heard the big door open and he said, 'Apartment six, yes?'

Somehow Erin must have said something in return, because he disappeared from view and she heard the heavy clang of the door far below. He would be coming up in the elevator now—which immediately made Erin think of another elevator, vastly more luxurious, when they'd almost

She heard the distinctive *ping* of the elevator's arrival and the doors opening.

He was literally outside her door now, probably wondering why she hadn't opened it yet.

There was a light knock. 'Erin?'

Erin felt slightly disembodied. Her brain had seized, as if protecting itself from thinking about the reality of what was happening.

She opened the door and had to adjust her gaze up. She'd forgotten how tall he was. And she was in bare feet, having kicked off her high heels as soon as she'd stepped through the door earlier. His impact hit her like a physical jolt through her body. Electricity crackled.

He frowned at her. 'Your hair is short.'

Erin lifted a hand and touched her head self-consciously. She'd had it cut a few months ago, because the baby had kept grabbing it.

She went cold all over. *The baby.*

Her hand dropped. 'Mr Nikolau...what are you doing here?'

He looked at her. '*Mr Nikolau?*'

Erin's hand gripped the door handle tight. She was beginning to recover some very necessary cognitive function. She realised she'd never actually referred to this man by his first name outside of the bedroom, because they'd gone straight from the boardroom to the bedroom with very little interaction in between.

She tried again. 'How can I help you?'

She would have asked him how he knew where she lived, but for a man like Ajax Nikolau nothing was a barrier to information.

Erin Murphy looked different with short hair, but no less attractive. The minute she'd opened the door and Ajax had seen her his entire body had clenched with recognition and need. Hunger.

He still wanted her. He'd never stopped thinking about her.

Even after almost two years. As each week had gone by, and then months, he'd been sure she would fade in his memory. She hadn't. But neither had that sense of panic he'd felt that she'd got under his skin on an emotional level. It had been strong enough to stop him from giving in to the temptation to seek her out again.

Until now.

Much to his irritation, no woman had managed to come close to making him feel the way she had. The two nights they'd spent together were engraved on his brain like a brand he would never be able to remove. He'd had many a sleepless night enduring X-rated dreams, waking hard and aching.

He'd resisted the memories and dreams for as long as he could. And life had helped in that respect. He'd never been busier. In the aftermath of the business deal of the century, Ajax's time had been monopolised by consolidating his position, in case anyone had any doubts he could pull his family's business together.

In the past year and more he'd silenced any critics or doubters. So much so that in the past couple of months he'd finally had time to take a breath and take his foot off the accelerator, and he'd realised that in spite of the many challenges he faced day to day, and the vast responsibility he had as CEO of Nikolau Industries, he was a little... bored. Jaded.

And, as if it had just been waiting in the wings for the right moment, the tantalising possibility of seeing this woman again had filled his mind. He'd told himself that the impression he'd had of her getting too close had been brought on by their amazing chemistry, nothing more.

She'd lost weight. He didn't remember her looking so delicate. Her shorter hair drew attention to the fine bone structure of her face. Her huge eyes. The long slim neck. Elegant collarbones visible under the neck of her silk shirt.

His body tightened. 'Can I come in?'

She didn't move. 'What are you doing here?'

Ajax, a man used to people allowing him access to wherever he wanted to go, realised that this wasn't proceeding as he'd envisaged. His arrogance mocked him.

'I'm here to see you.'

'Why?'

The blunt question reminded him of how she'd been able to cut through a lot of waffle and point people towards what was important. She'd been good at her job. He missed that.

Before he could speak, voices became audible in the corridor behind him and Erin seemed to make a split-second decision.

She stood back. 'You'd better come in.'

The offer was ungracious, but Ajax wouldn't object. She was flushed in the face, and that made him think of how she'd looked under him as he'd joined their bodies.

He looked away from her and around the apartment, to try and regain some control. It was airy and bright. Homely. Books on shelves. Throws on a well-loved couch. Something about it caught at him, in his chest, creating a kind of yearning. Disconcerting...

'Mr Nikolau—'

He looked back at Erin, a little more in control of his faculties. 'Really? You're going to stand on ceremony?'

Her mouth tightened. 'It was almost two years ago, and a very brief...thing.'

Thing. That was one way of describing it. It had been a conflagration that had moved Ajax to cut it off, starve it of oxygen, for fear that it would run rampant. But if he'd let it do that then maybe he wouldn't be here now.

'I think the time for ceremony has come and gone. Please call me Ajax.'

Erin's jaw gritted momentarily. Then she said tightly, 'Very well, Ajax. What can I do for you?'

'I understand why you might have felt the need to resign from the law firm, but you didn't have to.'

Erin went pale. 'You...want me to work for you again?'

Ajax's conscience pricked. His motive for coming here was far more ulterior and earthier. 'I hear you're doing well at your new firm. Certainly your old boss misses you.'

'You've come all the way here to tell me I was a valued employee?'

Now his skin prickled with a sense of exposure. He wasn't used to people questioning his motives. He wasn't used to questioning his own motives. But he'd made this journey without really thinking it through—not like him. He was behaving like some sort of homing pigeon, guided by forces beyond its comprehension or control.

Erin was looking at him, waiting for a response, once again reminding him of how forthright she was. Her eyes were beautiful, brown and green, ringed with long dark lashes.

It struck him then that he was here because he was looking for some sort of connection—something he hadn't felt since he'd been with this woman.

Erin still couldn't believe Ajax Nikolau was standing in her small one-and-a-half-bedroom apartment talking to her. Saying…nonsense. She needed him to be gone. This situation was too dangerous. She wasn't ready to let him know he was a father right now. She had intended to go to him and be cool and collected. Calm. Not in her stockinged feet with her baby—*their baby!*—just feet away.

Before she could think of something appropriate to get him to leave, he asked, 'Why did you leave the law firm? Because of what happened between us?'

Erin swallowed. She wasn't about to explain her emotional vulnerabilities to the man who had been responsible for them.

She managed to force out, 'Don't be ridiculous. I took my new job because it offered better prospects.'

Then he said, 'I haven't had a lover since you.'

He sounded almost accusing. He was looking at her intensely, the same way he had in that elevator. Blood rushed to her skin, making it tingle. Between her legs she pulsed with awareness and it shocked her. She hadn't felt so much as a blip of desire since the baby.

Since Ajax.

She was confused. She was afraid to think too much about what it meant that he hadn't had a lover since her. Or how that made her feel. Slightly giddy…

Erin tried to ground this rapidly evolving situation in some reality again. 'Why are you here?' She was confused. Did he want her to work for him?

Ajax shook his head slightly, as if clearing it. 'I think I

came here because I haven't forgotten what it was like...
Have you?'

As if to help her, a memory flashed back of how it had
felt to have Ajax's body moving in and out of hers, skin
slick with sweat, hearts pounding, straining to reach the
building pinnacle of—

'Yes,' Erin lied desperately. 'I've had other things to
think about.'

Like his daughter.

Her guts churned as memories of finding out about the
pregnancy flooded her brain.

She'd thrown herself so completely into her new job,
to try and put what had happened between her and Ajax
Nikolau behind her, that three months had almost gone by
before she'd acknowledged the bouts of morning sickness
that had lasted for about a month, and noticed that her already irregular periods had actually stopped.

And that the bloating wasn't going away. In fact, it was
getting worse. She could barely fit into some of her clothes
any more.

And when yet another male client's gaze had gone to
her bigger than usual chest she'd had to face the fact that
she ought to take a moment out of her schedule to get her
symptoms checked.

Until the doctor had said those fateful words—*'You're
pregnant, almost thirteen weeks along'*—she'd literally not
even contemplated that possibility. Or maybe she'd been
too scared to let the possibility exist.

She had a mild form of endometriosis, so whenever
she was irregular or there were strange symptoms she
put it down to that. And stress had always had a big effect on her periods, too, so to say finishing an affair—

even short-lived—and starting a new job was stressful was an understatement.

The doctor had looked at her incredulously. 'You really had no clue?'

Erin had shaken her head, feeling stupid.

Pregnant.

She'd been in a daze for days.

Ajax's voice cut through the memories as he said, 'You're not married or engaged?'

Erin covered her hand. 'That doesn't mean anything. I could be in a relationship.'

'Are you?'

She'd forgotten how blunt he was. *'Just so we're clear, I want you, Erin.'*

She shook her head. 'No…but are you really suggesting that there's still something between us?'

He didn't have to answer that. It sizzled between them, as much as Erin would like to deny it

Desperately she tried to pretend it wasn't happening. 'Do I need to remind you that you were the one who cut things off?'

'Maybe I was a little too…hasty.'

The memory of how close she'd allowed him to get made Erin say tartly, 'It's been almost two years—the opposite of hasty, I would say.'

His gaze met hers, and the intensity of his unusually light eyes made Erin quiver inwardly.

He said, 'I've been a little busy.'

'Well, so have I.'

Birthing his daughter.

Tell him.

But her mouth wouldn't form the words. Guilt was like acid in her stomach.

Ajax took a step closer to Erin. She knew she should step back, but her limbs were like lead.

He said, 'How can you deny it when it's running like electricity between us right now?'

His scent washed over her and she breathed it in—distinctive and achingly, instantly familiar, musky and woody with something spicy underneath. It hurtled her back in time and all Erin could see was Ajax. She was engulfed in memories and, treacherously, lust. The stresses and strains of the past months dissolved. She was just a woman again, standing in front of the man who had seared himself onto her psyche in more ways than one.

She'd really felt as if she'd been reconfigured after those two nights in his bed. Her cells realigned. Even though she hadn't been an innocent, she'd felt as if he'd transformed her into a woman. A sexual woman. With a sense of her own sensual power. He'd given something to her—something she couldn't even name—but it had felt precious.

She'd forgotten about it until now. Or maybe she'd blocked it out. But here, under his avid gaze, she was feeling all those things again. Sensual. Powerful. Desired.

He reached out and touched her hair lightly. 'It suits you.'

Erin felt self-conscious. 'I… Thank you.'

Ajax kept his hand lifted, said, 'May I?'

Erin wasn't sure what he was asking, but everything in her body had her nodding her head.

His fingertips traced the line of her jaw, down to her chin. He lifted it slightly, looked at her mouth. 'I've dreamed of you…'

Erin had been too exhausted to dream much, but there had been nights when she'd known she'd had torrid dreams. She'd just been relieved not to remember much about them.

She'd felt them lingering in her body, though, because she'd woken aching, feeling unsatisfied.

Ajax moved closer. Erin didn't step away, even though she knew she should. Right now she couldn't quite remember why. She was caught up in the intensity of Ajax's proximity and the way he was looking at her, and so when his head lowered towards her and his mouth touched hers she felt nothing but a wild surge of desire.

Yes, please.

Had he asked if he could kiss her? She didn't care. She'd given her assent just by accepting it. His mouth moved over hers, more insistent. Asking a question. Erin answered without hesitation, her mouth opening under his, allowing him to deepen the contact.

He moved closer, wound an arm around her back and pulled her into him, so she could feel the hard thrust of his desire for her. It sent arrows of need right to her core, where she was melting, and—

Ajax pulled his head back abruptly. 'What's that sound?'

It took a second for Erin to register the cry of her baby. She reacted instantly, pushing free of Ajax's arms, and ran to the bedroom.

Ashling had pulled herself up and was standing in her cot, crying. She stopped as soon as Erin appeared, giving a gummy smile with glimpses of her newly formed teeth—undoubtedly the cause of her distress.

Erin went in and picked her up. Her cheeks were hot—a classic sign of teething pain. She'd almost forgotten about Ajax, so she was startled when she turned around and he was in the doorway.

Ashling saw him and went still in Erin's arms.

He was looking at the baby, his face like stone. Then he

stepped back from the doorway so Erin could come out. She had no choice. She went into the sitting room.

Ajax looked at Ashling again. And then, after a long moment, at Erin. 'You said you weren't with anyone.'

'I'm not.' She clutched Ashling to her like a shield.

He looked at the baby again. 'Who…? What?'

Reaction was starting to set into Erin's body. She felt herself trembling. 'Her name is Ashling.'

Ajax was transfixed. The resemblance between father and daughter was almost laughable as they studied one another. Olive skin…dark hair.

He dragged his gaze away from the baby to look at Erin. He said, 'She's mine.'

It was emphatic. But even though Erin knew this was her opportunity to admit that he was right, she heard herself blurting out, 'How can you be so sure?'

Ajax was grim. 'Because she's the image of my son.'

CHAPTER TWO

AJAX WAS HOLDING on to the edge of the kitchen island as if that could help anchor him in the midst of the storm surging around him. Belatedly he saw baby paraphernalia that he hadn't noticed the first time around. A bottle steriliser, teething rings, toys. A high chair. They mocked him now. Erin had taken the baby back into the bedroom to try and put her down again.

A baby. His baby.

He knew she was his as he knew his own name. She was the image of Theo at that age. Theo, his deceased son.

Ajax had spent so many of the recent years trying to block out the past, but now it was hurtling back with all the devastation of a bomb going off inside his brain.

His ill-fated marriage had been to a woman who had never been meant for him because she'd been promised in marriage to his older brother. It had been an arranged, strategic marriage, between two of Greece's most notable families, so when his brother had died tragically Ajax had taken his brother's place.

Sofia, his wife, had already been pregnant on the wedding day, and for appearances' sake Ajax had agreed that the baby would be named as his.

In fact he'd been his nephew. But Ajax had loved that boy

as if he was his own son, and Theo had known only Ajax as his father. A small, sturdy boy, with a mop of dark curly hair and bright mischievous eyes, he would grab Ajax's hand with his own little pudgy one, 'Papa, come see!' and he'd drag Ajax off to look at a snail or a frog in a pond, or the latest toy he was obsessed with.

The devastation of Theo's loss was suddenly acute all over again, making a lie of the cliché that time healed all wounds. Time would never heal that wound.

Ajax had grieved for his wife too, even though there'd been little love lost between them. Her death, and Theo's, had thrown into sharp focus how they'd been treated like commodities by their families. Coming from one of Greece's oldest and dynastic families, marrying a woman purely for duty's sake had always been Ajax's destiny— he'd never been under any illusions that love existed after witnessing his parents' loveless marriage and lack of loving parenting—but the reality of the cold and hollow experience of his marriage had only confirmed his cynical world view, and that he wanted no part of such a charade again.

Hence his all-out conquest of the family business, so that he would be the one calling the shots.

Ajax heard a noise from behind him and steeled himself. This visit to indulge his curiosity and his lingering lust for Erin Murphy had morphed into something else entirely. Something unwelcome and life changing. He had a child. A daughter. When he'd vowed after Theo's death never even to contemplate having another child. Yet it had happened. And Ajax couldn't process the full magnitude of that right now.

He turned around. Erin was gently closing the door to the small bedroom.

Even now, in spite of this bombshell, he couldn't stop

his gaze from roving over her body, or stop his response. It made his blood volcanic, a mix of shock, anger and desire.

He looked at her. 'Why didn't you tell me about my daughter?'

Ajax's stark question landed in Erin's gut like a cold, heavy stone. It had been a shock to hear him mention his son. It was no secret, the awful car accident that had taken his wife and son's lives some years ago, but he never spoke of them publicly and he and Erin had certainly never delved into such personal territory during their brief affair.

She couldn't speak for a moment, but then she said weakly, 'I did try…a few times…'

She was still reeling at the reality that Ajax was here, that he now knew about his daughter, and that their kiss had proved he still held a power over her that she couldn't fathom or control.

He frowned. 'When?'

Erin forced her sluggish brain to work. 'When she was about five months old, I called your office— they said you were in Greece. I didn't have a personal number for you. Obviously I couldn't leave a message with that information.'

In spite of their intimacies.

That drove home even more to Erin how inconsequential she'd been in his life.

Ajax's face was like stone. 'You said you tried a few times. That's once.'

'I wrote you a letter.'

Ajax looked as if he wanted to laugh. 'A *letter*?'

She nodded. 'I figured that would be as good a way as any to get the message to you.'

'Everything is electronic now. Letters are all but obsolete.'

Erin felt defensive. 'Yes, I'm aware of that. But as I no

longer had a company email address, I knew that any email I sent would most likely end up in spam. Or it would be opened and vetted by an assistant. I thought a letter would be safer and more private.'

His expression changed for a second, and then he said a little stiffly, 'Actually, that wouldn't have made much difference, they open all correspondence even if it's marked private. I have nothing to hide, and I have a policy of my staff immediately destroying any such correspondence. A woman making a claim that I'm the father of their child is unfortunately seen as an easy way to get some kind of engagement with men in my position. It works more effectively when the man in question is more promiscuous than I am.'

His words came back to her. *I haven't had a lover since you.*

Erin folded her arms, shutting out that reminder. So one of her messages could have got through, only to be thrown out before he'd even seen it. 'Well, in this instance it was a genuine claim—isn't that ironic?'

Ajax's jaw clenched. 'Did you try again?'

Erin nodded. 'I went to your offices one day, to try and see you—shortly before the birth. But before I could even give them my name I started to feel pains… I was going into labour.'

The colour left Ajax's face. 'You went into labour with my child in my building and I had no idea?'

Erin nodded, swallowing. He looked… She couldn't even decipher the expression on his face.

But then his expression blanked and he said, 'I'm sorry I wasn't aware. How did my staff not notice?'

Weakly she had to concede, 'That wasn't their fault. I was wearing a big coat—it wasn't necessarily obvious that

I was pregnant. But…as you might appreciate… I was occupied with a newborn after that, so telling you wasn't high on my list of priorities.' She finished, 'Those were all the attempts I made.'

'So were you going to try again…? When, exactly? In another year, maybe?' Ajax's tone was ascerbic.

Erin squirmed inwardly. She knew she deserved this. 'No, I knew it had to be soon.'

About three months ago she'd prepared to make another attempt to contact Ajax, but then she'd seen him in the paper, in the society pages, pictured at an event with a beautiful woman. The urge to contact him had dissolved—she didn't like to admit that she'd been jealous. And yet if she believed what he'd said here today, he hadn't taken another lover. So he hadn't slept with that woman…

His voice cut through her circling thoughts. 'Well, wasn't this timing serendipitous?'

'That's one way of looking at it.'

He emitted a frustrated sound, and then, 'I'm not royalty, Erin. I'm not that hard to contact. It wasn't as if you would have been a stranger trying to contact me.'

'True. But you made it very clear after our last…meeting that no further contact would be welcome.'

The sting of that rejection was as painful and vivid now as if it had just happened. He'd said, *This was a mistake. It won't happen again.*

Erin pushed down the old pain. She couldn't afford to let him see that vulnerability now.

'That was before I knew you were pregnant,' he pointed out.

She countered, 'I didn't know you hadn't received the letter. I assumed you had, and that you weren't interested in your daughter.' *Or me*, she didn't say.

'Of course I would have wanted to know. I'm not made of stone.'

A flash of heat went through Erin's body. She knew very well that he wasn't made of stone.

She brutally slammed down on that reminder.

'Look,' she said, 'I'm sorry again that I didn't get to let you know before now. I could have tried harder. But the truth is…it wasn't just because you were hard to contact.'

Ajax frowned. 'What are you talking about?'

Erin swallowed before divulging, 'My mother left me and my father when I was still a toddler. Just walked out. I've only seen her since then sporadically. When I believed you'd got my letter and had ignored it I thought you were rejecting Ashling. It made me less inclined to pursue telling you. Obviously I would have… But I didn't want her to be rejected the way I'd been. And then,' she said, 'there's what happened to your family.'

There was instant tension in the air. Ajax said, 'What are you talking about?'

'Your wife and son who died. I thought maybe that was the reason why you mightn't want anything to do with another child.'

Ajax looked incredulous. 'I had a right to know, in spite of what happened in the past. There's a difference between choosing to have a family again and an unplanned pregnancy.'

Oof. That landed in Erin's gut like a punch. And it shouldn't. Their passion had burned bright and hot for a very brief moment. That was all it had been. A moment. An aberration. A man like this would never have chosen a woman like her to have his child. He came from a Greek dynasty. She came from second-generation immigrants. Her father and mother had been the first in both their families to go to university.

Erin lifted her chin. 'Yes, you did have a right to know, and I've explained my side of it. You might remember what it's like with a newborn? I'm sorry to mention it but—'

Ajax put up a hand, every line in his body tense. 'Then don't.'

Erin closed her mouth. She'd been right about his son, but it was no comfort.

Ajax was still rigid with reaction at the mention of his son. Her words *'You might remember what it's like with a newborn'* had precipitated a slew of images and memories of holding the soft weight of Theo in his arms as he'd walked him up and down, getting him back to sleep. The wonder of that small form and the immensity of awe he'd felt. Like nothing he'd ever experienced.

He shook his head, as if that might dislodge the painful images. He had to focus on the present moment. *His daughter.* And how it had happened and what they were going to do next.

'We used protection.' He couldn't help but sound accusing.

'I know…it obviously failed. I hadn't expected this either—believe me.'

'Who takes care of her while you work?'

Erin's eyes flashed, as if she resented being asked the question. *Well, tough.*

She said, 'My father sometimes—he had her today. Or I leave her in a creche that is right across the street from where I work.'

'How old is your father?'

'Sixty-eight.'

At Ajax's obviously sceptical look, Erin said defensively, 'He's physically and mentally very sprightly.'

'It's not ideal.'

'No, it's not. But it's all I can afford right now, as I'm only working part-time.'

Ajax's mouth was tight. 'I could have been supporting you.'

She lifted her chin. 'You once accused me of playing games to get your attention. I support myself and I can support my child.'

'Who is also *my* child,' Ajax pointed out.

Erin suddenly blanched, as if she was fully realising that Ajax was now here and knew that he had a daughter. He might have almost felt sorry for her if he hadn't still been reeling with the full extent of this news himself.

The sudden blast of a siren outside reminded him of something. He glanced at his watch and cursed silently. He looked at Erin. 'I have to go—I have a business dinner this evening. But we're not done talking about this.'

Erin said, 'I can meet you when it's convenient.'

Ajax held out a hand. 'Give me your phone.'

She retrieved it wordlessly from her bag on a chair, unlocked it and handed it over. Ajax gave it back after a few seconds.

'You have my number now. Text me so I have yours. I'll be in touch.'

Within seconds Ajax was gone, seemingly taking all the air in the room with him. Erin went to the window and opened it, sucking in a deep breath. She saw Ajax emerge onto the street below and cross the road, and how the driver hopped out to open the back door of a his car. Ajax slid in and the gleaming silver SUV moved away into the Manhattan traffic.

Erin let out a shuddery breath. So now he knew.

He still wants you.

She shook her head to negate that assertion. He might have come looking for her on a whim, but there was no doubt that the discovery of a daughter he'd known nothing about had doused any desire he still felt.

Erin turned from the window and sent a simple text to Ajax.

Erin.

She got one back almost immediately—a terse acknowledgement.

I'll be in touch.

She had no idea what to expect next. She didn't really know Ajax Nikolau at all. In spite of their intimacies. In spite of watching him at work over those intense few weeks. He was as good as a stranger. A stranger who was one of the most powerful men in the world.

And the father of her child.

She was bound to him irrevocably, for life, no matter what happened. But she was determined not to let Ajax upend their lives to suit him. Whatever was coming, she would be prepared.

'Mr Nikolau is ready to see you now.'

Erin took a deep breath and stood up. It was strange to be back in the building where she'd worked with Nikolau's legal team. And where, a few floors above them, she and he had—

No, not going there now.

She straightened her suit jacket and flicked an invisible speck of dirt off the silk shirt that was tucked into slim-fitting pencil trousers. She couldn't look more professional— even if she was quivering inwardly. The briefcase she carried felt as if it weighed a ton, even though it only held paper.

Ajax's assistant opened the door to his office, standing back to let Erin through. The woman had barely acknowledged Erin, apart from saying the minimum required to greet her and ask her to wait for a few minutes.

Erin stepped over the threshold and it took her a minute to orientate herself. She'd forgotten how big his office was. He was standing at the very far end, near a massive desk, in front of windows that took in a truly intimidating view of downtown Manhattan.

He was wearing a shirt tucked into dark trousers. No tie. Sleeves rolled up. It was one of the things that had appealed to her about him from the start—he was a man who was happy to get stuck into things. It had surprised her, because men at his level usually left it to their minions to do the work, but he'd wanted to be over every little nut and bolt of the negotiations.

And now that memory struck a shard of fear into her. Would he be the same when it came to his daughter? It had been a week since she'd last seen him. He'd sent a curt text the day before yesterday, telling her to give him a couple of options of times for meetings, and now here she was.

The sun was setting over Manhattan behind him, bathing the iconic city in a golden light. But all Erin could see was him. Tall and formidable.

'Come in.'

What had seemed like a great distance between them now felt minuscule as Erin crossed the luxuriously carpeted floor. She stopped at the other side of the desk. He couldn't have looked more stern and remote. A million miles from the charming man who had come to her apartment to seduce her again. Now his light eyes were like two chips of ice. She felt it in her blood. Making her cold.

A moment stretched between them, taut with tension. But Erin wasn't going to say anything until he spoke.

Eventually he asked, 'Who is minding the baby?'

The baby.

Her hackles rose. 'Her name is Ashling and she's with my father—her grandfather.'

'A name that until a week ago I'd never even heard before.'

Guilt struck Erin again, like a little piercing needle. 'It's Irish…it means dream.'

He didn't seem particularly impressed by this. And then, as if remembering his manners, he offered, 'Would you like something? Water? Coffee?'

Erin's throat suddenly felt as dry as sandpaper. 'Maybe just a little water, please.'

She watched as he came around from behind the desk and walked with loose-limbed grace to the drinks cabinet. He poured her a glass of water and brought it back. She plucked it from his fingers as quickly as she could, afraid that her skin would touch his.

As it was, she was battling flashbacks to that second night, when they'd had an impromptu midnight feast in his kitchen. She'd laughed when it had become apparent that he didn't know where basic things were in his own kitchen.

They were a long way from that moment now.

She took a sip of water. Ajax went back behind his desk. He put out a hand, 'Please, sit down.'

Erin shook her head. 'I'm fine standing.' Then, before her nerves could consume her, she blurted out, 'What are your plans?'

He'd had a week to absorb the news and think it all over...consult with lawyers. Erin was acutely aware of that.

A muscle in Ajax's jaw pulsed. 'My plans are to discuss how we proceed from here.'

Erin swallowed. He sounded terse. Angry. He had every right to be.

'For what it's worth, I'm sorry again that you had to find out the way you did. That I couldn't get a message to you sooner.'

He said, 'There's no point going back and forth over a past we can't change, we need to think about the future.'

Erin's gut clenched. Ajax was in no mood to be concilia-tory and she couldn't blame him. She was in this situation and had to deal with it as best she knew how.

She said, 'I agree, to that end, I've drawn up a legal doc-ument, if you'd like to see it?'

Ajax focused on the woman in front of him, who was tak-ing a sheaf of papers out of her briefcase, head bent. He was momentarily glad not to be looking into those far too mesmerising eyes. One second brown, the next green, and then gold. They were too distracting. Too perceptive. They made him forget what was happening here. The huge be-trayal of her not telling him about his daughter.

He wasn't sure what he'd expected today, but Erin tak-ing legal documents from her case, as if this was a busi-ness meeting, was definitely not a scenario that had come into his head over the past week.

She was looking at him now and holding a sheaf of papers over the desk towards him. He took it, bemused. Glanced at it. It was entitled: *Custodial and Visitation Agreement between Ajax Nikolau and Erin Murphy.*

She said, 'First of all a DNA test needs to be done to establish paternity.'

Ajax put the contract down. There was a needling sensation at the back of his neck. Normally he was the one who took others by surprise.

'I know she's mine.'

'I appreciate that, but it's for your benefit. Without legal confirmation that she is yours, you don't have any rights to claim paternity or custody.'

She shouldn't have had to remind him of that.

The needling sensation got stronger.

He said, 'And presumably you wouldn't have the right to demand paternal support?'

Erin's face flushed. 'There are no *demands*. She will be entitled to support from her father the same as any child. I can support us quite well, in any event—'

'On a part-time attorney's salary?'

She flushed even darker now.

Ajax found it beyond satisfying to see this evidence of emotion. Satisfying and arousing. He cursed his weakness.

'I have other means,' she divulged, a little hesitantly.

Ajax arched a brow.

With obvious reluctance she elaborated. 'My mother sent me a monthly allowance until I was eighteen. I put every cent into savings. I never intended to use them unless absolutely necessary, but they're there. I own my apartment outright. I'm not here to look for anything outside of fair maintenance, and to establish some ground rules for custody and visitation.'

Ajax heard the pride in her voice and thought of the fact that her mother had left her. Against his better intentions he felt a tug of empathy. His parents might have been more physically present than her absentee mother, but they might as well have been absent for all the actual parenting they'd done.

This woman had intrigued him from the very first moment he'd seen her. She still intrigued him. The fact that he couldn't say in any moment what she would do was... refreshing, when he was used to people contorting themselves into pretzels to do what they thought he wanted.

What was *not* refreshing, though, was how she affected him. He was used to being surrounded by the most beautiful women in the world, and yet it was this one—uniquely—who seemed to have infiltrated his body and mind in such a compelling, comprehensive way that he only wanted her. Even now, after the bombshell discovery of the daughter she'd kept from him.

He said, 'Obviously I'll have to go through this with my legal team.'

'Of course. I'd expect nothing less. But I think you'll find it very reasonable.'

Curious now, he said, 'Give it to me in broad strokes... what you've set out.'

'Once your paternity is confirmed, I've proposed a child maintenance payment system until Ashling is an adult, depending on whether or not she goes to university, until such time as she's graduated.'

That prospect made Ajax feel slightly winded for a moment. He had an image of a tall, slim, dark-haired woman, smiling, with a mortarboard cap on her head. He hadn't even imagined that for Theo.

'Go on,' he bit out, regretting having asked the question now.

'Her life will be here, with me, and I will be her primary carer. But you will be permitted access regularly. Holidays can be negotiated too. I recognise that she will have family in Greece. I want her to have a relationship with you, and the other side of her family. Both my parents were only children. I don't have aunts, uncles or cousins.'

Ajax turned and walked to the window, taking in the vast view of downtown Manhattan without really seeing it. He had legions of cousins and aunts and uncles, but they might as well have been inanimate statues for all the warmth or affection he and his brother had ever received from any of them. Cousins had been pitted against one another in annual get-togethers that had had more resembled *The Hunger Games* than a fun family occasion. Rivalries had been fostered, not friendships.

He knew from what Erin was saying that that wasn't what she envisaged at all. She had no idea what his family were like. He'd told her he wasn't royalty, but in many aspects, when it came to marriages and bloodlines, his family behaved as if they were.

She said from behind him, 'One thing is non-negotiable. If you don't intend to foster a relationship with her—a *real* relationship, with regular meaningful meetings—then I must ask that you simply provide financial support and step back. I will not allow inconsistency—it's not fair. You're either in, or out.'

Meaningful meetings.

Like his relationship with Theo.

As someone who had never really known love, and certainly not unconditional love, having a child had taken Ajax unawares, and before he'd had time to protect himself it had been too late. He'd fallen in love with his son. Who hadn't even been his son. Loving Theo had broken Ajax wide open, leaving him exposed and vulnerable.

If that was what love was, he had a better understanding now of why generations of his family had had arranged marriages and kept their distance from their children. Because the pain of losing Theo had destroyed him.

It had killed something fragile and nascent inside him. It had mocked him for believing he was deserving of love… that he might experience something so pure.

The toxicity of generations of calcified emotions was what he knew. Not something as unbridled and outrageous as actual real emotion. He'd learnt that lesson the hardest way possible.

And yet here he was, being offered another chance to destroy himself all over again. His daughter might not suffer a tragic accident—Ajax knew instinctively that Erin was a conscientious mother, unlike his deceased wife—and that she would do her utmost to protect her child. *Their* child. But no power on earth could promise that no harm would come to her.

The thought of embarking on a relationship with his daughter and living with the terror of losing her every day almost made Ajax's legs buckle. He broke out in a sweat. His heart started to thump irregularly. Panic filled his veins.

He couldn't do it. Couldn't put himself back in that place of losing himself to a greater force only to have it snatched away from him like a punishment. He'd seen the child. She would be impossible *not* to love. Cherish. Protect.

She would do far better without him. Without this terrifying strangulating fear in his veins. After Theo, Ajax knew he couldn't endure such pain again. Loving or losing.

That was why he'd vowed to himself that he would never try to have another family.

'Ajax?'

He forced down the panic. The fear. He said, to his own reflection in the window, 'I had a child and I lost him. I won't go through that again.'

'But—'

Ajax turned around. Steeled himself. 'Non-negotiable.'

Erin closed her mouth. She obviously sensed that this was not a moment to push it. She'd clearly seen something on his face.

Eventually she bent down and pulled something else out of the briefcase. A small padded envelope. She put it on his desk.

'This is the DNA self-test kit. You need to take a swab from inside your mouth and package it up, then send it over to my doctor. All the information is there. He has Ashling's DNA sample already. Once they're matched, you're her legal parent.'

Ajax walked back towards the desk. He felt a heavy weight in his chest.

Erin said, 'So, are you saying…you don't want to be involved?'

He forced himself to look at her and said, very clearly, 'That's exactly what I'm saying.'

CHAPTER THREE

'BA-BA-BA-BA-BA…'

Erin smiled at Ashling, who was cooing and babbling to herself in the bath as Erin washed her. Ashling loved water.

A small plastic duck went flying. Erin caught it and handed it back so she could throw it again. But her mind kept looping around and around Ajax's final devastating pronouncement after their meeting the other day.

He didn't want anything to do with his daughter.

Erin felt guilty. Had she pushed him into a corner where he'd felt he had no choice except to push his daughter away?

Obviously losing his son had had a huge effect on him. More than Erin had appreciated. She got it. The thought of anything happening to Ashling made her feel dizzy with fear. But to let that inhibit any future relationship with a child…? Erin couldn't understand that.

Maybe it wasn't just grief for his son. Maybe Ajax had realised that he really didn't want children. After all, it wasn't as if Ashling had been planned—as he'd pointed out.

Erin deftly plucked her out of the bath and dried her, dressing her in her nightclothes before giving her her evening milk. Ashling was tired. They'd been in the park for the afternoon with Erin's father. She went down with only the smallest objection, falling asleep in spite of herself.

Erin traced her daughter's plump cheek and then let herself out of the room. Evenings like this were rare, and she was grateful after the turbulence of the last week.

Erin hadn't yet had the heart to tell her father that Ajax had rejected his daughter at the first opportunity. He was just happy that Ajax now knew.

Even though Erin was desperately disappointed with Ajax's reaction, on some deep level it didn't surprise her. After all, she knew well the capacity of a parent to leave their child.

When Erin's mother had left her, she'd also walked away from her husband—Erin's father. He'd confided in Erin that he'd wanted a family and that her mother had not. But when she'd fallen pregnant with Erin, her father had hoped for the best—only to watch in despair as his highly intelligent and academic wife had become more and more suffocated by the domesticity of having a child.

Eventually she'd left, choosing herself and her academic career over being a mother and a wife, scoring a deep wound inside Erin.

It was only since she'd had Ashling that Erin had felt that wound start to heal. But along with that had come more pain. Because now that she knew what it was to be a mother, and to feel that ever-expanding humbling love, she understood even less how her mother could have abandoned her the way she had.

How cruel was it that she'd unconsciously chosen a man who had the same ability to walk away from a child as her own mother? She smiled at herself humourlessly. No doubt a psychotherapist would tell her she was still playing out her childhood trauma, and looking for someone to heal that wound. Well, she'd failed at the first hurdle.

The DNA test results had been delivered to Erin by courier that morning, confirming what she already knew. Ajax Nikolau was Ashling's father. He would have received the results by now too, and it obviously hadn't precipitated a change of heart as she'd heard nothing from him.

Her daughter was destined to grow up—as Erin had—without the love and presence of one of her parents. It would be up to Erin and her father to shower Ashling with all the love and confidence-building support they could.

Erin woke the next morning not to her daughter's unintelligible babble, but to her phone ringing on her nightstand. She looked at the clock. It was early. She saw the name *Ajax* and came instantly awake, sitting up in the bed.

'Hello?' Her voice was rough with sleep.

Ajax was terse and to the point. 'Something has happened. We need to talk. Can you arrange for the baby to be looked after? I'll send a car for you in an hour.'

Erin struggled to take in what he was saying. Luckily her father lived only around the corner, and he was always up early.

She responded, 'I… Yes, I guess so. I'll let you know if there's—'

But Ajax had terminated the call. Erin looked at her phone in astonishment.

How rude.

An hour later her father was pushing Ashling out through the main door of the building in her pram. Erin said a hurried goodbye and went to the blacked-out SUV waiting for her by the kerb. The driver was holding open the back door, and as she approached he said, 'Good morning, Miss Murphy. I'm to take you straight to Mr Nikolau.'

The streets of Manhattan at this hour were still relatively

quiet. Erin wondered what on earth was going on to make Ajax behave in such an urgent manner.

She wouldn't have to wait long to find out.

The car pulled up outside his building and she got out. An assistant led her into the elevator. The same elevator where she and he had combusted. Her cheeks started to burn, but luckily the serious assistant wasn't looking at her.

The elevator opened straight into Ajax's apartment, as it had done both times she'd been there. Morning light flooded the luxurious space. It still looked unlived-in. She couldn't imagine letting Ashling crawl around on these undoubtedly priceless carpets, leaving sticky handprints everywhere.

And then suddenly he was there. In dark trousers and a light shirt. Top button open. Hair a little messy, as if he'd been running a hand through it. Jaw dark with stubble. He hadn't shaved yet.

It made Erin think of that last morning, when she'd woken to find him dressed and looking at her with a grim expression. Shaved jaw. Making her feel very disheveled.

'I'm sorry I couldn't come to you. I've been tied up here with calls and I had to speak to you as soon as possible to get ahead of everything.'

Erin's brain still felt a little sluggish. 'Ahead of…what?'

'Come with me,' Ajax said as he turned around again, and then he asked, 'Do you want coffee? Anything to eat?'

'Coffee would be great.'

It might help her wake up and not feel as if she was dreaming. Another assistant said she'd bring it through, and Erin barely had time to say how she liked it before Ajax was disappearing down a corridor.

She hurried after him, deliberately ignoring the door that she knew led into his bedroom.

She found herself following him into a large corner room that turned out to be a home office. There were books on shelves, multiple computers, screens showing various images and information. A TV built into the wooden panelling was showing a news channel on mute.

The assistant materialised with Erin's coffee. She took it gratefully and noticed that she closed the door behind her.

Ajax's scent had caught at her as soon as she'd seen him. Woody and earthy, with something that was deeper...spicy. Uniquely him. Very male. Every nerve-ending in her body was humming with awareness, in spite of her best efforts to remain immune.

Erin took a quick gulp of coffee in a bid to be more alert. Even though she knew any desire he'd had for her had died, she wasn't sure she could trust that she wouldn't betray herself, alone in a room with him. Their history in that regard hadn't exactly been without incident.

She took a moment to acknowledge that she felt very underdressed. Ajax and his assistants looked as if they'd been up for hours. She'd just thrown on a pair of sweatpants and a matching top after a quick shower before she'd woken Ashling. She'd let her hair dry naturally, and could imagine it was sticking out all over the place.

Ajax was looking at a screen, and then he stood up straight. 'You need to see this,' he said.

Erin felt a clench of trepidation at the expression on his face. She put her cup down on the table and went around the other side of the desk to stand beside him.

It took her a moment to take in what she was seeing. A slew of lurid headlines and...

She bent to look closer and put her hand up to her mouth. There was a picture of her, with Ashling in her buggy, and it looked as if it had been taken yesterday, when they'd been coming back from the park. There was even a picture of her kissing her father goodbye.

The headlines were all a variation on *Who is Nikolau's mystery baby-mama? Baby joy for tragic Nikolau! Second chance for happiness! Will Nikolau put a ring on it?*

Erin stood up straight again. For a moment she felt dizzy. 'What…what is this?'

'This,' said Ajax, sounding as grim as he looked, 'is the result of someone on my team leaking news for personal gain.'

Erin backed away until she came up against a hard surface. She went around the desk again, wanting to get away from the pictures and the headlines. For someone who'd never merited so much as a blip of a mention anywhere outside of academic notices, and who had no social media, this evidence of invasion into her privacy felt like a physical violation.

She could almost feel the colour leaching from her face.

Ajax looked at her and came around the desk to take her arm. 'Sit down.'

She did. Her legs were wobbly. He handed her some water. She took a sip. Put the glass down. Tried to get her head to function. Ajax was pacing.

She said, 'I hadn't even thought that far ahead…to the public knowing about you and the baby…but obviously it would have happened at some point.'

Or maybe not, she rebuked herself.

Hadn't he said he wanted nothing to do with her? Maybe he would have denied being her father. It was the way it sometimes happened in celebrity circles, and then there was always a very public spat to force acknowledgement…

'Erin?'

Ajax was looking at her. She said, 'What did you say?'

'That I'm sorry. I never intended it to come out like this. I was planning on announcing it far more discreetly and ensuring that you would both be well protected from the inevitable ensuing interest.'

The relief that he had intended to acknowledge his daughter, even if he still couldn't seem to bring himself to use her name, was almost as destabilising as seeing those headlines.

He continued, 'But now it's out, and any attempt to control it will be like trying to put out a raging wildfire. By now there will be people in every newsroom tasked with finding out who you are and your entire life history.'

That didn't bother Erin too much.

She shrugged. 'They won't find anything of interest.'

Her most outrageous behaviour had been in an elevator with this man. Her cheeks started to burn again. She took another quick sip of water.

As if she hadn't spoken, Ajax was saying, 'You'll be hounded. You'll have to leave your apartment and go somewhere else.'

Erin *did* mind that. 'We can't just leave. Everything we need is there. And my father is just around the corner.'

Ajax looked at her. 'Your father won't escape their scrutiny either.'

'He's a professor of advanced mathematics,' Erin offered dryly. 'I'm sure they'll lose interest quickly. Surely if we hole up for a day or two they'll lose interest?'

And then, even as she said that, she thought of the intense interest Ajax attracted whenever he appeared in public. The constant speculation if he was pictured with anyone. She'd been one of those people poring over his image recently, wondering who his date was, if it was serious.

He shook his head. 'It'll take longer than a couple of

days. The photographers who took those pictures yesterday won't be so discreet from now on. They're probably gathering outside your building right now.'

Erin shivered at the thought of being at the centre of such scrutiny.

'And it's not just you. It's the baby.'

Something cold went down Erin's spine. 'What do you mean?'

'Now that it's out who she is, she's a target.'

'Why?'

But even as she asked, Erin knew. She was the secret daughter of one of the richest men in the world.

Ajax was pacing again, saying almost to himself, 'If I'd had time I would have made sure you were protected, but now...' He turned around. 'I'm due to go to Greece today for a month. A mixture of work and social events.'

Erin frowned. 'Why are you telling me this?'

'Because there's only one solution, to contain this story and make sure you're both safe. You and the baby are coming to Greece with me.'

CHAPTER FOUR

ERIN COULD SEE the heat shimmering over the brown landscape as they descended onto an island bathed in the golden light of the rising sun. It was one of the Cyclades chain, strung like jewels across the Aegean Sea.

There were darker patches of green, and bright splashes of blue and turquoise lakes emerging from the volcanic earth. Villages appeared in clusters on hills and closer to the coast, distinctive with their white and blue paint. And it was all surrounded by the sea in varying shades of green and blue.

Ashling was sleeping…a heavy weight in Erin's arms. Her first time on a plane and she'd been amazing. Erin could hear the low rumble of Ajax's voice behind her, talking on the phone or with his assistants, who'd accompanied him for this leg of the trip. Apparently the staff would be travelling on to Athens after this flight, while Erin and Ajax went to the Nikolau villa.

She'd tried to resist this dash across the planet to escape a brewing media storm, but when she'd seen the throng of media outside her apartment building she'd had to concede that Ajax had a point. And what had really swayed her was the thought that Ashling would become a target for media interest and, worse, the potential danger of kidnap.

She'd managed to get a weekend call with her boss and had explained that there was a family emergency and she wasn't sure how long she'd be away. If she was gone for longer than two weeks her pay would be docked, but as she was only part-time her absence shouldn't cause too much of a ripple.

Her father had helped her to pack and get Ashling ready for the journey, and then they'd been collected by Ajax's driver from the back of the apartment building, giving the media the slip. They'd been on a plane within hours of Ajax's dawn wake-up call.

Erin was glad she'd at least had a chance to change into something other than sweatpants. Now she was wearing soft faded jeans and a loose linen shirt. Slip-on sneakers. She'd no idea what she'd packed—she'd been more concerned with making sure she had all Ashling's things.

The flight attendant came down the aisle to prepare them for landing. Erin buckled Ashling in without waking her. She'd been fed and she was in her night clothes—hopefully she would sleep again once they'd got to the villa, as it was still their night-time.

Ajax had assured her that his team would have prepared their rooms before arrival and ensured she had all the necessary requirements for Ashling. Erin didn't doubt it. In Ajax's world, things materialised and happened as if by magic. She wouldn't be surprised to see an exact replica of the nursery from her own apartment recreated in his villa.

But, apart from making sure they were comfortable at the start of the flight, Ajax hadn't come near them. Erin was beginning to see how his 'hands-off' approach might work, and it was as disconcerting as it was effective.

She hated to admit that she was still so aware of him.

The plane landed and Ashling woke with the *thud*. Predictably, after being so amenable, she was now cranky and tearful. It had been a long day.

Ajax appeared when the seatbelt sign went off. He was wearing his suit jacket again, and looked annoyingly fresh, as if he'd slept in the vast bedroom at the back of the plane. But Erin knew he hadn't. He'd worked the whole time.

She felt a little sorry for his team. But then, she'd once been one of them.

Not going there now.

She stood up, holding Ashling, who curled into her.

Ajax said, 'Okay? How is she?'

Erin noticed that he barely glanced at Ashling.

'She's been great, but she's still tired and I can sense a storm brewing. How long will it take to get to the villa?'

'Only about fifteen minutes. Think she can last that long?'

'She'll be fine.'

The heat hit Erin as soon as they stepped out of the plane, like a wall, even at this early hour. Ashling's head came up and she stopped whinging, as if she was sensing she was back in the land of her ancestors.

Erin could only imagine what it would be like later in the day. Insects were loud in the grass on the other side of the runway.

She was vaguely aware of officials greeting Ajax and documents being checked. The perks of travelling with a billionaire.

An assistant led her over to a sleek silver SUV and opened the back door. There was a car seat for Ashling. Erin secured her in the seat and gave her a teething toy to chew. Then she got in on the other side and sat beside the baby seat.

It was only when no driver appeared, and she saw Ajax

peel away from the assistants and officials to stride towards the car, that she realised he was driving them himself. He shucked off his jacket before he got in, and Erin couldn't help her gaze moving over his broad shoulders.

She was sitting behind him, to his right, so she could see his eyes in the rear-view mirror.

Suddenly feeling a little light-headed at the speed with which they'd traversed the globe, she asked, 'Is this villa your family home?'

Ajax shook his head, taking a road heading away from the airfield and small airport. 'No, I bought it years ago—for myself.'

'Where did you grow up?'

'Athens, mainly, when I wasn't at boarding school in England and then Switzerland.'

'How old were you when you were sent to boarding school?'

'Eight.'

Erin gasped. 'So young...' She couldn't imagine packing Ashling off at the age of eight to go anywhere.

Ajax shrugged lightly. 'My older brother was there already.'

'Were you close?'

Erin saw Ajax's eyes in the mirror, his gaze narrowed on the road in front of him. 'Yes and no. Our parents encouraged us to compete more than collaborate.'

Erin absorbed that. 'Your parents are still alive?'

'Yes.' Terse. And then, as if conscious of Erin's silence, Ajax added, 'They're in Athens. We also own some islands, and they pick and choose where to go for holidays or family events. Or they travel to their other homes around the world.'

'Family events...? Are there many of those?'

'There's one in a couple of weeks.'

He was avoiding meeting her eye in the mirror. Erin didn't have to ask him if his family knew about Ashling—it must have hit the papers here too by now. She wondered how the news had gone down. She was beginning to suspect a certain level of conservatism and snobbishness...

'Ah-gab-bab-dada...'

Erin smiled at Ashling who was looking out the window and pointing to the sky.

A sensation on the back of Erin's neck made her look up to find Ajax looking at her through the mirror at last. Instantly she was warm and tingling. The hairs on her skin were standing up. She couldn't look away, and eventually he did.

He was a good driver—fast, but safe. Not showy. Erin was acutely aware of his hands on the wheel. Big and strong. Masculine. She remembered how they'd felt on her. Not soft. Firm. Possessive. A pulse throbbed between her legs. She cursed herself.

She could see they were approaching a village, with houses strung along the road. Bright red and pink bouganvillea spilled over walls and roofs. It was quiet at this hour of the morning. Fairy lights were strung over doors and between buildings. Erin could imagine them lit up at night. It was unbelievably pretty.

But Ajax kept going a short distance out through the other side of the village, until he turned abruptly down a narrow track which then opened out again revealing iron gates and a wall on either side.

A man emerged from a security hut.

'Kalimera,' Ajax greeted the man, and they conversed for a moment before the gates opened and they drove up along a wide drive bordered by flowering plants on both sides.

Erin could see pristine green lawns. And then her breath was taken completely when they drove around a bend and the driveway opened out into a huge courtyard with a fountain centrepiece, and a two-storey villa appeared before them.

The rising sun bathed the building in a bright glow, the pale and weathered stones of the villa making it almost fade into the background. It looked majestic, but also warm and rustic. Erin wasn't sure what she'd been expecting, but it had definitely been something more modern—perhaps stark white with sharp edges.

This was warm and inviting and beautiful, and it made something in her chest tighten. As if she'd had a dream of this image but hadn't realised it till now.

Ajax opened the car door and for a moment Erin felt almost superstitiously that once she stepped on this land her life would change for ever. *She* would change. But she was being ridiculous. She got out, avoiding Ajax's eye, not wanting him to see how this place was affecting her already.

There was a small breeze, bringing scents of the sea and wild herbs and plants.

Ashling emitted a cry from the car, a demand for attention, and Erin hurried around to take her out of the seat and hold her in her arms. A woman appeared in the massive front doorway, beaming. She was dressed in black, wiping her hands on an apron.

She greeted Ajax in rapid-fire Greek. He was smiling at her. The tightness in Erin's chest intensified. She hadn't seen him smile since their last night together. And she hated it that it mattered to her.

He looked at Erin. 'This is Agatha, my housekeeper. She lives on the property with her husband, who is the caretaker.'

Erin nodded at her shyly, and to her surprise the older

woman came over and immediately held her arms out for
Ashling, who went quite willingly into them, as if she knew
this woman.

'We will have some milk, yes? And maybe a change
of nappy?'

Erin was surprised to hear her speak English. She started
to say, 'I think she's okay, actually—' but the woman was
already disappearing into the villa with the baby.

Erin felt a bit stunned. 'She still needs the right milk—'

'I ordered ahead for all your requirements. You gave
my assistant a list.'

Erin looked at Ajax. 'That was only on the plane.'

'She called ahead. Agatha has had six children. She'll
be fine.'

Erin felt impotent all of a sudden.

Ajax said, 'Let me show you around.'

She felt that if she protested she'd be overreacting, so
she followed Ajax around the side of the villa and up some
steps to a terrace with a wall that overlooked a vast lawn.
There was a swimming pool in the distance, just visible
behind a wall of bushes, and just as she was thinking it
was a potential hazard for a very curious baby who could
crawl at the speed of light, Ajax pointed to the gate acting
as a barrier between the terrace and the lawn.

'She'll be quite safe…don't worry.'

The fact that he'd thought the same thing at the same
time was some comfort.

French doors were open into a sumptuously decorated
reception room which led into a formal living room and a
dining room. The kitchen was on the level below, huge and
gleaming. There was a home gym down here too.

Back upstairs, Ajax showed Erin another informal living
room, complete with a massive screen for watching TV or

movies and a sound system. Books on shelves... The latest magazines...

Then they went upstairs to the bedrooms. Ajax indicated to where the guestrooms were located—too many for Erin to count—and then moved down another corridor. He stopped outside a door and then pointed to the end of the corridor. 'That's my room, down there. This is you and the baby.'

Erin was about to remind him of the baby's name, but he was opening the door and Erin stepped into the most beautiful room she'd ever seen with the softest carpet underfoot. A warm off-white on the walls with a gold trim. Simple but elegant furniture. A huge four-poster bed, muslin drapes held back by silk ties. White linen that looked so inviting it just reminded her how sticky and tired she was.

And hungry, she realised, just as Agatha appeared in the doorway with Ashling in her arms, who saw Erin and immediately leaned towards her mother, cribbing a little.

Erin took her and cuddled her close. She smelt fresh. 'Thank you, Agatha, you didn't have to change her.'

'No problem. Come and see the nursery—you let me know if you need anything.'

Erin followed her to an adjoining door. The nursery was a plain room, with one of those circular cots that Erin had always coveted but hadn't been able to afford.

Agatha was saying, 'We didn't have time to decorate, but it'll be done by the end of the week.'

Erin noticed lots of things in boxes, but there was a changing table, and supplies of nappies and creams and wipes. A nappy bin. A chest of drawers stuffed full of more clothes than Ashling would ever be able to wear.

The suitcase Erin had packed with Ashling's things looked very shabby in this pristine space.

Agatha pointed to a monitor on the chest of drawers. 'Yours is in the bedroom, beside the bed. Its range will cover the whole property, so you'll hear if she makes a squeak.'

Erin hadn't needed baby monitors up to now, as her apartment was so small.

Agatha said something to Ajax in Greek, and he nodded and said, *'Efharisto.'*

Agatha left and Ajax turned to Erin.

'Please, make yourselves at home. Agatha has prepared some breakfast on the terrace downstairs for you, and then you'll probably need to sleep for a few hours. I noticed you didn't get much rest on the plane.'

He'd noticed? But at the mention of food, her stomach rumbled. Classy. She blushed.

'Okay, that sounds good.'

'I have some work to catch up on. I'll come for you before dinner this evening, after you've had a rest.'

Even though he'd worked all the way through the flight clearly Ajax wasn't at the mercy of such human failings as needing to rest.

He was still looking at her, and she said quickly, 'Yes, of course, that's fine. You don't need to entertain us.'

'It's no problem. I'll see you later.'

Ajax left and Erin let out a long breath. She looked around. The French doors were open onto a small balcony. She walked out and took in the view of lush rolling gardens. The sky was lighter now, losing the golden touch of dawn. The heat was rising too. She could hear the faint splash of waves in the distance. The air was scented with a mix of flowers and sea and grass.

It was paradise.

Ashling's head was tucked into Erin's neck. She was exhausted. Erin made her way downstairs to the terrace and put Ashling in a highchair, feeding her bits of fruit and pastries while she helped herself to the same.

Once she and Ashling had eaten, she thanked Agatha and made her way back upstairs, where Ashling went down with minimal fuss. A sign of her exhaustion.

Once the baby was fast asleep, Erin left the door to the nursery ajar and turned on the baby monitor, then checked the other one was on. It was so sensitive she could hear Ashling's breaths.

She explored further, to find a dressing room with all her things already unpacked. Were there other staff here apart from Agatha? Invisible? She wouldn't be surprised. It seemed all too magical.

Then there was the bathroom, with its footprint about the same size as her entire apartment. There were two sinks, a bath the size of a small pool, and a huge shower. Honey-coloured tiles... Exclusive beauty products and a large fluffy robe...

Erin couldn't resist washing the stickiness of the journey off her body and she stripped off on the spot, before stepping under the steaming spray of the shower. It was bliss.

After drying herself, she kept the towel wrapped around her and lay down on the soft bed. She fell into a dreamless sleep.

That evening, even though she was expecting it, Erin still jumped when there was a light knock on the bedroom door. *Ajax*. Her heart thumped at the thought of seeing him again. *Pathetic*.

Luckily she *had* packed appropriately, and she was wearing a plain shirt-dress, teaming it with a leather belt and flat sandals.

At the last moment she'd resisted reaching for any make-up apart from some tinted moisturiser. She'd left her hair to dry naturally. Dinner with Ajax wasn't a date.

She checked quickly that Ashling was still asleep and that both monitors were on, before taking hers with her. She took a breath and opened the door—and nearly melted on the spot.

Ajax was wearing faded jeans and a dark polo shirt. Short sleeves. All she could see was how his biceps bulged under the material. His skin was bronzed and gleaming. He made her feel very pale and washed out. She cursed herself for not making more of an effort. He must be wondering what he'd ever seen in her.

'Ready?'

Erin nodded. She left the door open and fell into step beside Ajax.

He said, 'She's asleep?'

Erin nodded. 'It took a while—her body clock is all over the place. We slept for a few hours this morning, and then I kept her occupied for the afternoon in the garden. Hopefully she'll sleep through to dawn. I'm lucky—she's a good sleeper.'

Erin felt as if she was babbling.

She slid Ajax a glance as they went down the stairs. 'Did your wife and son spend much time here?'

He shook his head, and when they reached the ground floor he put out a hand to indicate which way to go. 'No, they were never here.'

Erin had a vague memory that the accident had happened in Athens.

They were walking out onto the terrace now. Night had fallen and candles were burning, imbuing the pretty space with a soft golden glow. A wrought-iron table was set with a white tablecloth, gold-trimmed crockery and silverware, sparkling crystal glasses.

Ajax pulled out a chair. Erin sat down. Ajax took his own seat. It suddenly felt very intimate.

A young girl Erin hadn't seen before appeared, smiling shyly as she filled their water glasses before disappearing again.

Ajax said, 'This island isn't owned by my family, so it's a better place to stay off the radar.'

Erin tried not to gape. 'You mentioned that your family do own islands?'

'A few.'

She'd bet that that was an understatement. She said, 'This is a beautiful place. It's a pity your wife and son didn't spend any time here.'

Ajax's expression was hard to read. 'My wife preferred life in Athens and on islands like Santorini or Mykonos,' he said. 'This would have been too quiet for her.'

Erin couldn't understand that. Who wouldn't want to come and relax in this idyll, away from the chaos of everyday life?

Before she could persuade him to talk more about his previous existence, the young girl appeared again, with two plates of simple Greek salad, crisp and delicious. The feta cheese was fresh and salty and creamy, the tomatoes ripe and juicy from the sun.

Ajax held up a bottle of chilled white wine and looked at her. She nodded her assent. He poured her a glass and she took a sip, letting it slip down her throat, zesty and perfectly dry.

She could feel it hitting her veins almost immediately, making her feel even more as if she must be hallucinating. She'd wake up soon, back in her apartment, with the sounds of Ashling waking up and the non-stop sirens outside.

She blinked.

Still here.

'You enjoy your food?'

Erin looked at her clean plate, and then back up to Ajax. She arched a brow. 'Not used to women clearing their plates?'

Totally unfazed by her jibe, he took a sip of wine, unhurried. *Sexy...* Erin pressed her thighs together. The delicate wine glass should have looked ridiculous in his hand, but it only made him look even more masculine.

The young girl took their plates and then returned a couple of minutes later with the main course. The smell was mouthwatering.

Ajax said, 'Moussaka made with beef—one of our most traditional dishes.'

Erin took a few mouthfuls. She hadn't realised how hungry she was, but she hadn't eaten much since breakfast, when they'd arrived.

The moussaka was perfect and light, in spite of the rich tomato sauce.

'Delicious,' she said to Agatha, when the woman came out to clear their plates.

The housekeeper smiled. 'My grandmother's recipe. How is the little one?'

Erin nodded towards the monitor, with its light spiking intermittently when Ashling made a move or a snuffling sound. 'She's fast asleep, thank you.'

When she'd left with their plates, Ajax leaned forward with the wine bottle, but Erin put her hand over her glass.

'Not for me, thanks.'

Apart from wanting to keep her wits around this man, she also needed to have a clear head for Ashling, who might wake during the night.

He poured himself another half-glass. Erin found herself blurting out, 'How long ago was it…? Your wife and son?'

Ajax put the bottle back down. His jaw was tight. Erin knew she was straying into territory he didn't welcome talking about, but she had a right to know. After all, Ashling was his son's half-sister.

'Five years ago.'

'I'm sorry. I can't imagine how devastating it was.'

He looked at her, and she almost gasped out loud at the pain in his eyes.

'It was the worst.'

Erin's chest tightened and something dark prickled in her gut—something that spoke of jealousy, because he'd obviously loved his wife so much and he hadn't rejected his first-born child.

Sensing he wouldn't welcome any further platitudes, she said, 'So what happens now?'

'I'll work from here for the next couple of days, to make sure that you and the baby—'

'Her name is Ashling,' Erin interjected. She was feeling prickly. This whole scene was too seductive, and she was so acutely aware of him, but they weren't here for a romantic interlude.

She was here under sufferance, because the press had found out about Ashling, and if that hadn't happened Erin had no doubt that Ajax would be in Athens, probably wining and dining another woman, not even thinking of her.

Here he was being civil. Yet not civil enough to refer to his own child by her name.

Ajax's expression was unreadable. A little stiffly, he said, 'I hadn't ever planned on this again.'

Erin hesitated a second, then said, 'But you planned it...before?'

Ajax looked at her. And then he took his wine glass and stood up. He went over to the stone wall, turned his back to her. Erin couldn't help her gaze moving over the width of his shoulders and then down to his narrow hips. Firm buttocks, lovingly outlined by the faded denim.

She looked away hurriedly, afraid he'd turn and catch her ogling him. But he didn't turn around. He said, 'Actually, no, I didn't plan it.'

'So...how...?' Erin trailed off, confused.

He turned around and rested his backside against the wall, looking at Erin. 'My older brother was due to get married and start a family. He and Sofia were the ones who were engaged. But a few weeks before the wedding he was on board one of our ships and a storm blew up. He was trying to help the crew when he slipped and hit his head. He never recovered and he died a few days later.'

'I'm sorry,' Erin said. To have the death of his brother and then his wife and son...it had to have been almost impossible to get over. But then she frowned, 'You said your brother was engaged to Sofia?'

Ajax nodded.

'How did *you* end up marrying her?'

'It was a strategic marriage, designed to forge a strong union between my family and hers. When my brother died she was already pregnant with Theo. It was agreed that I would marry her—to protect the agreement between the families and to minimise the gossip about Theo. But it's a relatively open secret that he was actually my nephew.'

This was huge. Too much for Erin to take in all at once.

'So you and she…?' Erin trailed off again.

Ajax arched a brow. 'She and I…what?'

Erin felt foolish for asking, but some part of her needed to know. 'You didn't marry for love?'

Ajax looked at her for a moment, and then to her shock he emitted a sharp laugh.

'Love? No. She wasn't marrying my brother for love either—although they were better suited. Physically, at least.' He continued, 'Sofia and my brother and I come from families where anything as frivolous as love was weeded out generations ago. Marriages are as strategic as business deals.'

So Theo hadn't been his son. His marriage hadn't been based on a love match, as Erin had assumed. For someone who considered herself to be healthily cynical, she felt exposed—and very gauche.

Of course men like Ajax Nikolau moved in very different circles. There was too much money and power at stake to merely fall in love. And yet she knew that losing Sofia and Theo had been devastating. Or at least losing Theo…

As if reading her mind, Ajax said, 'I don't—' He stopped and amended his words. 'I *didn't* consider Theo a nephew. He was my son. I was there for his birth. I had no idea what to expect, but when he was handed to me…'

'You fell in love?' Erin said quietly.

He looked at her, and she could see even now the slightly bewildered expression on his face. 'Yes, I did.'

No wonder he'd decided never to risk it again. Loving and losing… She could understand it now, even if it didn't make it any easier to accept.

She wasn't so different herself. The thought of loving someone enough to be hurt by them was terrifying to her.

Witnessing her father's devastation had been almost worse than her abandonment by her mother.

After her one relationship at university she'd realised that focusing on her career brought her more satisfaction, and no man had come along to distract her from that or persuade her otherwise. Until Ajax. It wasn't that she wanted to emulate her mother's obsession with work above all else, but more that she didn't want to risk the devastation she'd witnessed growing up with a heartbroken and lonely father.

She forced her mind away from such concerns. There was no danger of that here.

Erin said, 'Her name is Ashling and she exists—no matter how much you want to distance yourself from that fact.'

Ajax's mouth tilted on one side in a rueful half-smile. 'I think that horse has bolted by now.'

It was something, and Erin clung to it. 'Thank you for telling me what happened. So, what is the plan?'

Ajax said, 'Like I said, I'll stay here for a couple of days, to make sure you and the—'

He stopped and Erin held her breath.

He continued, 'To make sure you and Ashling settle in okay.'

Hearing him say his daughter's name was seismic. Erin wanted to thank him, but that would be weird.

She thought of what he'd said and then shook her head. 'You don't need to stay—we'll be fine. We can walk down to the village if we need anything.'

'No.'

Ajax's voice was sharp, and he'd straightened up. Erin could see his knuckles white around the glass. He seemed to notice his own tension and relaxed a little.

'Sorry, but there's no need to leave the villa. I'll make sure you have everything you need.'

Erin frowned. 'We're not allowed to leave?'

Ajax looked irritated now. 'If you need anything you can ask Agatha to get it for you—or her husband.'

Erin stood up and said slowly, 'I know you don't mean to keep us here as prisoners. And, while it is beautiful here at the villa, I like to go for walks. And Ashling will need stimulation. When we drove through the village I thought it would be a nice place to go for morning coffee, or lunch.'

His face was like stone.

Erin tried to push down a lurch of panic. After all she was half a world away from home, with a man who she really didn't know that well at all.

'Ajax, what is it? Surely we're allowed to move around freely? We're not in danger here?'

His expression softened. 'No, of course not. It's just...' He swept a hand through his hair, clearly agitated. 'Sofia and Theo died because she insisted on driving into Athens. She wouldn't let a driver take her in spite of my requests.'

Her panic subsided. Ajax didn't strike her as a control freak, so perhaps there had been more to it. And his son—*nephew*—had died in that crash, so perhaps he had a right to feel a little paranoid. It clearly meant that he felt protective over Ashling, whether he wanted to admit it or not.

Carefully, Erin said, 'Okay... Well, I can't drive. I never learned because it wasn't necessary. I grew up in one of the busiest cities in the world, so I think I can handle a sleepy Greek village, but if it makes you happier someone can drive us in and out and I will keep you informed as to our whereabouts.'

Ajax said, 'That's...fair.' And then, 'I didn't know you couldn't drive?'

Erin made a small face, 'Well, actually, I can. But I

just never got around to doing my test. A car is a burden in Manhattan.'

The night was soft and fragrant around them. Warm. No sounds from inside. Had Agatha and the young girl gone to bed?

A wave of weariness washed over Erin. She picked up the baby monitor. 'I think I'll go to bed now. It's been a long day.'

As she was turning to go, Ajax said, 'Thank you for trusting me enough to come with me.'

Erin stopped. She hadn't even considered that she'd trusted him enough to let him derail their lives within hours. Yet she had. More or less without question. She felt exposed now, even though she knew that all his reasons for leaving New York were very valid and compelling.

She faced Ajax. 'How long do you think we'll have to stay here?'

'A few weeks at least.'

Even though she'd cleared the absence with her boss, and she was still only part-time, she hoped for a more per-manent position as Ashling got older. She didn't want to push the firm's generosity.

'If it's any longer than that I'll have to clear it with work.'

'I'm sure something else will have materialised in the news by then, and the vultures will have moved on. By the time you return to New York they'll no longer be in-terested.'

Erin was about to turn away again when Ajax spoke again.

'But I think there is something that we can do to nip any further speculation in the bud for good.'

'What's that?' she asked.

Erin already knew she wasn't going to like his answer.

'Appear together.'

'As in…where? How?'

'In public. As if we're a couple.'

CHAPTER FIVE

AJAX KNEW HE should be feeling mildly insulted at the look of abject horror on Erin's face, but then he was becoming used to her reactions around him being the opposite of what he might have expected with other women.

She looked tired. His conscience struck. He remembered what it was like with a baby. He'd done a lot of the waking at night when Theo was small. Those had been some of his favourite moments, just him and Theo in the dark, walking up and down while the world slept. Those huge eyes on him, as if he held all the secrets of the universe. And yet he hadn't been able to keep him safe...

Suddenly he felt as if Erin could see all the way down inside him, to where his guts hadn't stopped churning ever since he'd found out about the baby. *Ashling.* His daughter. The thought of holding her and looking into her eyes made him feel clammy with something he didn't want to name.

He said, 'You know what? Let's leave it till the morning. It has been a long day and I'm keeping you up.'

'I'd prefer to know what you mean now.'

Ajax cursed himself. He should have kept his mouth shut. He'd been trying not to notice Erin too much all evening, but it was impossible.

She couldn't be dressed any more plainly—a shirt-dress

and bare legs, sandals… Patently little make-up. Her hair slightly messy and rough from drying naturally. And yet she couldn't have been more alluring. Her eyes were huge. Golden-brown. Serious. But when she smiled…her whole face lit up.

Not that he'd given her much cause to smile since they'd met again.

Since he'd discovered his secret daughter.

A spark of anger helped him to focus on what he had to say and not on her. For a moment, at least. Although what he was about to propose was going to throw him all the way into the fire unless he exerted every ounce of control.

He said, 'I had a meeting with my PR team on the way over here. They pointed out that if we're photographed together to coincide with this news of a baby, then it'll take some of the heat out of the press interest. But if we're not seen together they'll dig and dig until they know everything there is to know about you.'

'What about you?'

Ajax shrugged. 'They already know everything about me. You're the unknown quantity. Being seen with me will protect you to a degree. There's little for them to get excited about if it looks like we're together after having a baby. We can spin it that we managed to keep it a secret.'

Erin looked suspicious. 'Can't we just hide away here and then go home in a few weeks, when it's all died down?'

The fact that she didn't want to be seen with him shouldn't be pricking Ajax's ego the way it was. She was right to want to protect herself from scrutiny. He'd been used to it all his life. From the moment he and his brother had been born they'd been watched and judged.

'I know what I'm asking—for you to put yourself under the spotlight—and it might seem contradictory, but by doing that just for a short time I do believe it'll have the desired effect of taking the heat out of speculation and rumour. Then we can release a statement saying we're no longer together. Although I will obviously always ensure that you and Ashling are protected.'

Erin sounded suspicious, 'When you say "a short time"... what does that mean?'

'While we're here in Greece. If you agree, we'll attend a few events.'

'What's "a few"?'

'Two or three in public...one with my family...'

Ajax was very aware of not letting his gaze drop to her bare shapely legs. He had a vivid flashback to pushing those legs apart—

No! The woman in front of him was the one woman on the planet he could not touch again. Things were already complicated enough. She was the mother of his child and he had no intention of playing happy families again. Under no circumstances.

He would take the heat out of the press's interest in Erin and Ashling and then they would get back to their own lives. He wouldn't abandon his daughter; she would be provided for as long as she needed it. And, as he'd told Erin, he would make sure they were protected. But he would not pretend that he could be a hands-on father again.

'Is it okay if I let you know in the morning?'

Ajax looked at Erin, his head still full of unwelcome thoughts. He nodded quickly. 'Of course—it's your decision.'

'Night, then.'

'Goodnight, Erin.'

He watched her leave, with the understated elegance that had caught his eye the moment he'd seen her. Then he cursed and turned around, placing his wine glass down on the wall. It was a wonder he hadn't snapped the delicate stem, he was so tense.

Bringing her and the baby here to this villa had been a bad idea. It was too full of memories of what he'd once wished for. Something that had been snatched from his grasp. The chance of a family—even with a wife who had been in name only.

Ajax hadn't ever expected anything more with Sofia. But he'd wanted to create a family with Theo. Do it differently. Be a proper father. Not treat his child as a pawn, to be moved around for the benefit of the family name and business.

The thought of actually fostering a relationship with his son had been audacious, because it was so alien to what he'd grown up with. No affection, no tactility. Tight, cold expressions. No love. The almost unbearable weight of a legacy so embedded in Greek society and lore that Ajax and his brother's lives had been mapped out before birth.

Clearly by buying this villa and making his dreams for a different existence concrete he'd angered the gods.

Ajax smiled mirthlessly.

He didn't believe in the gods, even if some people joked that his family line was so old they were descended from them. But he did believe in not being foolish enough to think that he could try again. Erin, and Ashling would be better off with him at a distance. The sooner the news interest died down and they could get back back to their lives in New York, under the radar, the better.

Ashling was already down for her mid-morning nap by the time Erin saw Ajax again. She was having a coffee on the terrace, with the baby monitor beside her. She'd been up with Ashling since dawn and she was tired because she hadn't slept well.

She'd taken in a lot of information the previous evening. All that stuff about the reality of Ajax's marriage and the fact that his son was really his nephew.

She'd also Googled herself and Ajax and what she'd seen had made her blood run cold. Lots of speculation as to who she was and how they had eluded the press before now. Questions asking were they together, and if not, why not?

She'd had to grudgingly admit that Ajax and his PR team were probably right. Give the media a little of what they wanted to see and the heat would die down.

A sound made her look up. *Ajax*. The object of far too many of her thoughts. He was dressed formally, in dark trousers and a white shirt...top button open. He looked fresh and vital, and not as if he'd spent a sleepless night. She wanted to scowl, but she forced a smile and ignored her pulse tripping.

'Morning.'

He looked at his watch. 'Almost afternoon.' Then he looked back at her. He noted the baby monitor. 'Napping?'

Erin nodded. 'She woke at dawn, so we had breakfast and explored the gardens a little.' Erin hesitated for a moment and then said, 'She's almost walking. Any day now.'

Ajax's expression didn't change, but it was as if he was consciously not allowing any titbit about his daughter to impinge upon him. 'That's good. There's lots of space for her to experiment here and not get hurt.'

'Yes, it's a big change from our apartment and the small park two blocks away. We could get used to this.' Erin had only been joking, but the minute the words came out she wanted to swallow them back. She said, 'I didn't mean that the way it sounded.'

Ajax waved a hand and came over to sit down, helping himself to a cup of coffee. A little dryly he said, 'I think you've proved that you're not bent on fleecing me of my fortune.'

'I wouldn't know where to start,' Erin admitted. She shrugged. 'I wasn't brought up to value money like that. We had enough to get by. I got a good education, went to university...that was enough.'

'You and your father?'

Erin nodded. 'As I said, my mother left when I was small.'

'You said you were a toddler?'

Surprised he'd remembered, she said, 'Pretty much, I'd just turned three.'

'But she supported you?'

'She sent an allowance that I put into a savings account. I wasn't going to touch it...but then when I got pregnant...'

'Your father is a professor?'

'Yes, of mathematics. His head is always in the clouds obsessing over formulas and problems to be solved.' Erin was smiling at the thought of her absent-minded father.

'You have a good relationship?'

She nodded. 'I adore him. It was just us. He was a good father, in his own scatty way. I was probably responsible ahead of my time, but I knew I was loved.'

Ajax shook his head. 'That's something rare in my world. Rarer than rare. A myth.'

Erin tried not to show how curious she was. 'Your parents...they weren't loving?'

Ajax let out a curt laugh. 'Loving? No. I don't think they even know the meaning of the word. Their marriage was arranged, and my parents have never pretended it was anything more. They've conducted discreet affairs on the side for as long as I can remember. My brother and I were brought up by nannies until we went to school—first in the UK and then in Switzerland as I mentioned. We hardly saw them, and yet our lives were beholden to their wish for us to follow the same path they had. A path of loyalty and dedication to a legacy that has become a massive global industry.'

'Didn't you ever want to do something else?'

'That was never really an option—and especially not after Demetriou died.'

'It doesn't sound like you're all that happy about it.'

Ajax's jaw clenched. 'I don't have the luxury of choice. Thousands depend on me for their livelihoods now. The company—as you know—has been restructured to give me more control.'

'Surely that's the opposite of what you really want?'

'It means my life is my own now. No one can put pressure on me to marry, or have heirs, or run the business by committee.'

'You have an heir. Ashling,' Erin pointed out, struck again by how adamant he was about not having another family. Or remarrying.

For a second Erin felt a jolt, thinking of him changing his mind some day and marrying someone else. She pushed it down. It shouldn't concern her. Their connection had been purely physical. At one point she'd felt as if her emotions were involved, but she'd convinced herself otherwise by now.

Ajax shook his head. 'I wouldn't let her get within a hundred miles of this business.'

'She might be interested.'

'If there's one thing I can do for her, it'll be to allow her to live her life under no pressure from me or this family. She'll have choices I never had.'

'Is that what you'd planned for Theo?'

Abruptly Ajax looked at his watch and said, 'Sorry to be rude, but I have to take a call. Did you think about what we spoke of last night?'

She'd touched a nerve, mentioning Theo, obviously. But she could understand why. She said, 'Yes, I did, and I think you're right. If we're seen together it'll cause some interest, but once they know how essentially boring I am it'll die down.'

Ajax frowned. 'You're not boring—far from it.'

Erin felt hot, and it wasn't from the sun. 'I don't usually behave in such a spontaneous manner...jumping into bed with people I hardly know.'

Not to mention making love in elevators.

'Neither do I.'

For a second, the air was charged. Erin was trapped in that blue-green gaze, and couldn't look away. He looked down, and her breath caught. Her breasts felt heavy, her nipples tightening under her thin top. A very plain thin top that suddenly felt invisible.

He looked back up again and Erin sucked in air. She felt as if he'd touched her. Just with his eyes. And yet she must have imagined the whole moment, mortifyingly, because he was looking at her with no discernible expression.

She tried to recall what they'd been talking about. Appearing with him in public...

'So...yes. Okay, I'll do what you suggested. Go out with you.' Heat climbed into her face. She sounded like a teenager.

'Okay. Good.' Ajax was brisk, further making Erin feel as if she'd conjured up that hot little moment. 'You'll come to Athens with me at the end of the week. We'll attend an event on Friday.'

'What about Ashling?'

'She'll come too.'

'But who'll look after her? It's only ever been me or my father or the crèche.'

'We'll hire a nanny.'

'Like the ones you had?' Erin knew that wasn't fair, but suddenly she had visions of a woman in uniform looking at Ashling disapprovingly.

A shadow crossed Ajax's face. 'No. Not like that. Agatha has family in Athens. I can ask her if she knows someone.'

Erin's fears subsided. She liked the woman—she was normal. Maternal. 'Okay, that sounds good. I trust her.'

'You only just met her.' He looked at her curiously.

Erin looked back at him. 'I'm a pretty good judge of character and she's kind.'

Before Erin could consider the fact that she was more or less telling Ajax that she'd judged his character and liked it enough to jump into bed with him—twice—she thought of something else.

'Is the event going to be very fancy?'

'It'll be black-tie.'

'I don't have anything formal with me.'

Ajax waved a hand. 'Don't worry about that. I'll have a stylist put together some choices.'

'I… Okay.'

Erin could hardly protest. And it wasn't as if she was going with him for romantic reasons. It was practically a job. Maybe if she looked at it like that it wouldn't feel so loaded?

At that moment there was a squawk from the baby monitor. Ashling was waking up. Erin stood up, glad her legs stayed steady. 'I should go. She'll be hungry for lunch.'

Ajax didn't say anything, but Erin felt his eyes on her

back and wished she was wearing something more exciting than her thin top and linen trousers. She usually prided
herself on feeling pretty well put-together, but under Ajax's
gaze she felt dishevelled. Unkempt.

The prospect of him seeing her in something other than
casual or work clothes made her heart beat far too fast. She
had to remember that these public appearances were purely
a means to an end. An end where their lives parted again
so he could carry on not engaging with fatherhood and she
could continue being a single parent.

A few days later, being driven through the streets of Athens after the relative idyllic peace of the island was a little
jarring, but Ashling was fascinated, staring out through
the windows in the back of the car as if she'd never seen
buildings before.

Erin felt a pang of regret that she hadn't made more of
an effort to tell Ajax about his daughter before.

The man in question turned to her from where he sat in
the front passenger seat. 'Not long now.'

Erin forced a smile, but her gut was churning at the
thought of what was ahead. She'd always been on the periphery of worlds like this—in the background, doing the
paperwork for titans of industry. Not front and centre under
the spotlight.

They were headed to Ajax's villa, in the hills overlook-
ing the ancient city. The Acropolis came into view, high
on its own hill in the distance. It humbled her. Yet another
reminder of Ashling's ancestry.

Athens was teeming with people—tourists and locals.
They'd passed through majestic Syntagma Square, and Erin
had caught glimpses of the narrow, cobbled streets of the

Plaka area. It was a beguiling city even as it baked under the sun.

But soon they were climbing up out of the city and into the hills. It became greener. The car stopped outside ornate gates that had appeared as if from nowhere, and a security guard in uniform opened up to let them in.

The driveway was long and winding, uphill, bordered by lush bushes until it opened out into a large courtyard area, revealing a sleek and modern split-level house. Sunlight glinted off the massive windows. It was in stark contrast to the more traditional villa on the island, but Erin liked it.

An attractive woman with glossy brown hair tied back into a ponytail, dressed in black trousers and a short-sleeved shirt, met them at the door. Ajax introduced her as his house manager, Marta. The woman was friendly, but serious…efficient. Clearly here in Athens things ran on a different schedule.

Then a younger woman appeared, pretty and shy, but smiling. She looked familiar, and it became clear why when Ajax said, 'This is Damia—Agatha's great-niece. She's going to help us with Ashling. She's studying English at college, and has plenty of experience in looking after babies as she has four younger brothers and sisters.'

Erin smiled at her and the girl immediately connected with Ashling, who smiled too, showing her emerging teeth. Erin felt a sharp pain near her heart to see how Ajax resolutely kept his gaze off his daughter.

Damia offered to take Ashling at once, so that Ajax could show Erin around. The little girl went happily, and Erin was simultaneously proud of how content she was and also piqued that she wasn't more clingy. But she knew to take advantage of these moments.

The villa was as sleek and modern on the inside as outside, but Erin was heartened to see that baby-proofing had already been undertaken, with the sharp corners of tables softened with pads. And the open-plan nature meant that Ashling would be able to roam pretty freely.

The living space, decorated with comfortable couches and chairs and coffee tables covered in glossy hardbacks, flowed into a formal dining space. Huge glass doors opened out directly onto a patio, which led to a pristine lawn sloping gently downwards to a row of trees behind which, Ajax told Erin, was a swimming pool and changing rooms.

The air was scented by the abundant flowers blooming on the edges of the garden. Erin wistfully thought of her father, who would immediately lose himself in identifying these exotic plants—a hobby of his.

Around to one side of the patio Erin gasped at the view of Athens laid out before them. The Acropolis looked like a toy replica in the distance. It was almost possible to make out the hundreds of people clambering over it like tiny ants. There were no skyscrapers or modern structures to ruin the view from this angle. It was truly impressive.

Back in the villa, she saw a baby gate had been installed on the stairs, ruining the architectural lines somewhat, but very necessary for a curious baby on the cusp of walking, who would soon be able to tackle stairs quicker than a flash of lightning.

As Ajax led her up to the second level Erin gestured to the temporary addition and said, 'Thank you for this.'

Ajax commented, 'I remember how it is.'

Erin followed him silently. He might not want to engage with his daughter, but he was already proving that he wasn't completely oblivious by taking such care over her safety.

Upstairs was elegant, with plush carpets and elegant minimal furnishings. Doors led off a long corridor and

Ajax opened one for Erin. She walked in and could hardly take in the scale of the room, it was so huge.

The bedroom, with a bed big enough for a football team, had two doors leading into an adjoining walk-in dressing room and then a bathroom that more resembled a spa. There was even a massage bed.

Yet another door Ajax had just opened led into a smaller anteroom which had been turned into a nursery, decorated with whimsical murals on the walls of dogs and bunnies and birds. Something struck her. Maybe…

She looked at him, but he seemed to read her mind and shook his head.

His voice was clipped. 'No, this wasn't Theo's. His and Sofia's rooms were elsewhere.'

One of the other doors they'd passed? She forced her mind away from speculating and took in the bright decor and the doors leading out to the wide balcony that ran outside the main bedroom too.

There was a cot and a changing table. A chest of drawers full of clothes from an exclusive French children's label.

She looked at Ajax. 'You didn't have to do this. She'll have outgrown most of these within a few weeks.'

'I wanted to make sure you have all you need.' He pointed to a door on the other side of the room. 'That leads into Damia's room, so she'll be right beside Ashling when we're out.'

When we're out.

As if they were a couple. But of course they were nothing like a couple. Couldn't be further from a couple. And that made her feel bereft—which was something she never would have expected.

Having a baby had changed her. She now knew that

deep down she hungered for companionship, and that she'd never put her career over that. Erin wasn't like her mother.

What about love? whispered a voice.

No, not love. Love had the potential to betray and destroy. Erin was realistic enough to hope for something that didn't have the power to wreck a life…a family. Since Ashling's birth she'd realised that some day maybe a family would be nice, with a partner she could like and respect. Trust. Companionship. Not the loneliness of her father's existence. She'd always longed for brothers and sisters—she'd like that for Ashling.

But that dream was shattering before it had even fully taken root. And it wasn't even Ajax's fault. He'd never promised anything. He'd never led her on. They'd had two hot nights when they'd connected with maximum physicality and minimum emotionality.

And yet here they were now, connected for a lifetime and having to navigate emotional territory that he obviously didn't welcome.

The sooner they got through these social events and defused the press interest, the sooner she and Ashling could get on with their lives. But a sobering realisation made her go cold. Their lives would never be their own again, no matter what happened. Ashling was the daughter of a billionaire and the whole world knew it. Ajax had even alluded to the fact that they may need security.

Feeling unsettled, she said to Ajax, 'Speaking of going out…the first event is tomorrow?'

Ajax nodded. 'Yes, in the evening.'

Erin's belly lurched. Being in this billionaire's world was suddenly all too real. She tried to hide her trepidation.

Ajax said, 'I've arranged for a stylist to come today, with a selection of outfits for you to choose from.'

Her belly was churning now. 'I know how to dress for work events—not high society. What if I wear the wrong type of dress?'

'Georgiana is very experienced. She'll know exactly what you need to wear.'

Erin couldn't help wondering if this *Georgiana* had dressed other women for Ajax. His wife? Even if he hadn't loved her, they'd have had to feel some affection for each other? Shared a bed at least?

'I…' What could she say? She'd agreed to this. 'Okay.'

'A statement will be put out by my PR team in advance of the event. That will hopefully nip most of the speculation in the bud.'

'I'd like to see it beforehand.'

Ajax arched a brow. 'To make sure it's legally acceptable?'

'Of course.' Erin couldn't stop her professional instincts from kicking in, even though she was fairly certain Ajax's team would be going out of their way to ensure the statement held no hint of a more permanent relationship in the near future.

'I'll have my assistant send you the draft copy.'

'Thank you.' Erin felt stiff and formal. The space was suddenly too small around her, as if all the air was being sucked out of the room. Ajax seemed huge. A solid wall of muscle.

'I should go and check on Ashling…she'll be getting hungry.'

Ajax looked at his watch. 'I have to go into my offices for a few hours. Go ahead and eat later without me. I'll find Damia for you and send her up.'

He left.

Erin went straight to the French doors and opened them,

sucking in a lungful of air. Had she made a huge mistake in agreeing to go along with Ajax's plan for them to be seen out together? That last exchange had been as chaste and civil as any conversation between two colleagues. He hadn't even touched her. And yet her skin was prickling all over, tight and sensitised.

It was so humiliating to still be attracted to the guy when he'd moved on so long ago...

'Miss Murphy?'

Erin whirled around to see Damia in the doorway, holding Ashling, who immediately put her arms out for her mother. She pushed all thoughts of Ajax and the future and how he made her feel out of her head and focused on her baby.

She smiled at the young woman. 'Please, call me Erin.'

CHAPTER SIX

THE FOLLOWING EVENING, Ajax stood at the bedroom door, where it was open just a crack. He felt like a voyeur, but he couldn't move a muscle. He was frozen at the vision of Erin, standing in front of the mirror, looking as stunned as he felt.

He'd always known she possessed an understated kind of beauty—the kind that mocked you for not noticing it at first. But now there was nothing understated about her... she was breathtaking.

She wore a strapless floor-length dress. Black. Its structured bodice-style design pushed her breasts up and cinched in her waist, and then the dress fell in soft silken folds to the floor.

Her skin looked very pale. She wore no jewellery apart from an elaborate diamond necklace and a matching cocktail ring. Luxuriant long black lashes framed smoky eyes. Blusher highlighted cheekbones so high and defined they could cut glass, and a nude gloss on her lips made them seem plump and provocative.

As if she was asking to be kissed.

Ajax was finding it hard to remember why that would be a bad idea.

Georgiana was talking to her. 'Your short hair really sets the look off. What made you decide to cut it?'

Erin replied, 'The baby…she kept tugging on it.'

Ajax tried not to let that image get to him, but it was hard. He remembered Theo pulling on Sofia's hair, and himself lifting him out of her arms when she got irritated. He couldn't imagine Erin getting irritated…

Georgiana said, 'Most women wouldn't get away with it but with your bone structure…'

Ajax could see that Erin was self-conscious, embarrassed by the praise. Again, not like Sofia, nor any of the women he was used to. They were born confident, expecting compliments, reveling in them. Erin looked as if she wanted the ground to swallow her whole.

Erin smiled at the stylist. 'Thank you for your help. I wouldn't have had a clue where to start.'

Georgiana winked. 'That's what I get paid the big bucks for.'

Ajax was about to knock on the door to announce his presence when Erin asked, 'Did you…er…work with Mr Nikolau's wife?'

'Sofia?'

Erin nodded. Georgiana shook her head, 'No, Sofia had her own ideas about style. She favoured a more modern aesthetic.'

That was a diplomatic understatement, thought Ajax. The two women couldn't have been more different. Sofia could have danced naked in front of him and he'd have felt nothing. Erin, on the other hand…

He slammed a lid on the surge of fire in his blood.

He knocked on the door and opened it, still not prepared when Erin turned around and his gaze met hers, gold and tawny. He was wearing a classic black tuxedo and he saw how her gaze swept down and up again, how a little flare of colour came into her cheeks.

He gritted his jaw.

Ajax forced himself to look at the stylist. 'Thank you, Georgiana.'

'My pleasure, Ajax. I'll be back when you need me again.'

Georgiana handed Erin a sleek black clutch bag and said, 'Good luck this evening—not that you'll need it. You're going to knock everyone out.'

Ajax was soon standing in front of Erin. She looked nervous.

'Is it…? Am I okay?'

He might not have believed it if he hadn't known better. He wanted to turn her around and put her in front of the mirror again. Say, *How can you not see how beautiful you are?* But he was genuinely afraid he might not be able to stop himself from tearing down that zip and undoing the exquisite picture she made.

Instead, he just said, 'You look…beautiful.'

'I feel strange. This isn't really me.'

'It is…for now.'

Until they were done with this charade and living separate lives again.

He said, 'My driver is waiting…we should go.'

As they walked downstairs, Erin tried to steady herself after seeing Ajax in his tuxedo. He oozed sophistication, but with an edge of sexy, brooding darkness that made her a little weak.

She wondered what he'd meant when he'd said *for now*. Did he mean just for this period of time, while they were acting out this charade of togetherness? And then, like Cinderella, she'd go back to her much less glamorous reality? She felt that was what he'd meant.

But Cinderella got her prince in the end.

Erin shook her head mentally. She'd never believed in fairy tales and she wasn't about to start.

In the hall, he asked, 'Do you need to see Ashling?'

Erin shook her head. 'Damia is feeding her, and then she'll bath her and put her down. It's probably best for me to go without drawing attention to the fact.'

'If we need to return at all we can, so don't worry about that.'

The little clutch of anxiety in Erin's chest eased. 'I think she'll be fine, but thank you.'

Ajax let her precede him out through the front door and Erin still felt wobbly in the delicate high heels. Her bare upper back prickled, as if she could feel Ajax's gaze on her.

The driver was holding the car door open. She got in, feeling awkward in the dress and shoes.

Ajax got in on the other side. The car moved down the hill and into the streets of Athens. It was early evening and the sun was starting to set, bathing everything in a golden glow. Tourists strolled easily, choosing somewhere to eat among the tables spilling onto the streets from cafés and restaurants. There was a youthful, vibrant atmosphere, a contrast against the ancient backdrop.

The car wound through the streets and then back up into the hills again. They joined a queue of cars entering gates like Ajax's villa's gates. Erin wondered if they'd gone in a big circle...

Ajax said, 'This is the Parnassus villa. Leo and Angel Parnassus are hosting their annual event to raise funds for charity.'

Erin had vaguely heard of Angel Parnassus. 'Isn't she a jewellery designer?'

Ajax nodded. 'Yes—very successful.'

'And Leo is…?'

'Like me, a Greek, who grew up mainly in America. We go back a long way. He returned here permanently some years ago, to take over the family business.'

'You lived in Greece while you were married?'

Ajax nodded, 'Yes, but America is my home now.'

He didn't elaborate. Erin speculated that perhaps the long distance from here made it easier for him to deal with the loss of his son.

They were at the top of the drive now, and the villa opened out before them. It was of a more traditional design than Ajax's. Vast, impressive.

They got out at the bottom of the steps leading up to the front door. Ajax took her by the elbow and Erin resisted the urge to pull away for fear he'd see how he affected her.

The sounds of soft jazz could be heard, and as they entered the hall behind other guests, a tall man broke away from a group of people and came over, a broad smile on his handsome face.

'Ajax! Please tell me you've decided to stop pretending you prefer Manhattan to Athens and are coming home.'

The men hugged each other warmly.

Ajax said, 'No chance.'

The man looked at her and Erin felt self-conscious.

Ajax said, 'Leo, this is Erin Murphy.'

Leo put out a hand. 'Erin, welcome to my home. And congratulations on your daughter. Our youngest is three, but maybe they'll play together some day.'

Erin couldn't help but smile at his effusive greeting. 'Thank you. I'm sure she'd love that. She's not walking yet, but any day now, I think.'

Leo made a face. 'Once they're on their feet you need eyes in the back and both sides of your head.'

Erin laughed. 'She's already crawling at the speed of light, so I know what you mean.'

She glanced at Ajax and saw he was looking at her with a transfixed expression on his face. Erin blushed.

A woman—stunningly pretty, in a white strapless column of a dress, with her dark hair pulled up into a classic chignon—came and joined them, sliding her arm through Leo's. She must be Angel. Her husband looked down at her, and his look was so full of hunger and love and tenderness that Erin felt like a voyeur. She'd never seen a man look at a woman like that…

After greeting Ajax with a kiss, the woman put out her hand to Erin. 'I'm Angel…so nice that you could come.'

Erin shook it. She noticed Angel's jewellery—a necklace of tiny diamonds strung on several interlocking delicate silver chains. She asked shyly, 'Is that one of your designs?'

Angel touched it and looked pleased. 'Yes, a new one I'm trying out. Do you like it?'

'It's lovely.'

Angel transferred her arm from her husband's to Erin's and led her away, saying, 'Then you must come with me, because these two wouldn't know how to appreciate art and design if it jumped up and—'

Leo protested. 'Hey, I've improved a lot.'

Erin let herself be led away by her hostess, charmed by her easy warmth and friendliness. They went into a huge room—a ballroom with gilt mirrors set into panelled walls and chandeliers hanging from an ornately decorated ceiling. Candles flickered from tall tables, imbuing everything and everyone with a glow.

Angel handed her a glass of champagne and said, 'A word of warning: be on your guard. I'm afraid that high society in Athens can be a little…cut-throat, and you've arrived on the scene with the biggest ace up your sleeve.'

Erin looked at her. 'What do you mean?'

'Ajax's baby. A baby no one expected him to have after… Well, you know.' Angel took Erin's hand and squeezed it gently. 'But I'm glad. He deserves to be happy. Theo showed him it was possible, but then it got snatched away.'

Someone approached Angel from the other side of the room and spoke into her ear.

She grimaced at Erin. 'Look, I have to run—but please, make yourself at home.'

She walked away, leaving Erin in the middle of the room alone. She looked around for Ajax, but couldn't see him straight away. As she turned she saw people stopping and looking at her. Whispering. Making little effort to hide their interest. She could see some of it was benign. But most of it was suspicious. Hostile. What had Angel said? *Cut-throat.*

Her hand gripped the glass of wine she held and suddenly she felt too hot. She walked towards the open doors that led out to a wide patio, where she could see more people milling around.

As she walked through the room she heard the whispers.

'She's some sort of ambulance-chaser lawyer…'

'She's not related to anyone…'

'She did it on purpose to trap him…'

'He's not going to marry her…'

Erin all but stumbled out through the open doors, and for a moment she was tipping forward perilously in thin air. Then a hand wrapped around her arm, steadying her. She recognised the familiar sizzle in her blood and looked up.

'Perfect timing,' she said. 'I'm sure they would have loved to see me go splat on my face.'

Ajax led her towards a low stone wall, beyond which

stretched stunning gardens and a panoramic view of Athens laid out before them.

He asked, 'What do you mean?'

Erin took a sip of wine and nodded her head towards the room full of people. 'Well, according to some I'm an ambulance-chaser, and I'm not related to anyone important, and—oh, you'll probably like this one—they don't think you'll marry me, so you're definitely off the hook there.'

Erin raised her glass in a mocking salute.

'I'm sorry. I didn't mean for you to be left alone.'

'It's fine. I was with Angel, but she was called away.'

Ajax's jaw clenched. 'This is why I don't like to live here full-time.'

'I guess Athens is a small enough city when it comes to this kind of thing.'

'Exactly.' He turned to her. 'By the way, the statement has dropped.'

Erin looked at him. 'The statement?'

'About us. To the press.'

The man addled her brain when he was close. No wonder these people thought she was just an ambulance-chaser.

She'd looked over the statement earlier and approved it.

Ajax Nikolau and Erin Murphy would like to announce that they have a daughter and are together. They ask for their privacy to be respected.

It couldn't have been more succinct.

Erin nodded. 'The statement... Yes.'

She looked up at Ajax again and her eyes widened. Had he moved closer, or had she? Even though they were outside, it felt as if she couldn't draw in enough oxygen.

'Considering the fact that almost everyone here is now looking at us,' he said, 'it might be a good moment to reinforce that statement with a display.'

'A display...?'

But Erin's words dissolved in her mouth as Ajax's fingers tipped her chin up a little, and then his head was lowering and his mouth covered hers in a light kiss. A light kiss that burned her all the way through to her core.

She wanted to lean into him, absorb his strength and heat, feel that heat surrounding her and his big hands moving over her. For a moment she was sure he wanted to deepen the kiss. His other hand was on her waist and she felt him tighten it, but then he pulled back abruptly and Erin opened her eyes to see him watching her.

A wave of mortification washed through her body. She was exposing herself spectacularly, but he seemed completely unmoved.

He took her hand and led her down the patio towards another door. They were going back inside to the ballroom.

Erin took her hand from his when they were among the throng again. He glanced at her, but she pretended not to notice.

'What is it, Erin?'

That sense of exposure was still prickling over her skin. 'I'd like it if you warned me in advance of any...touching or kissing.' She knew she sounded unbearably priggish, but the way she'd wanted to cleave to him at the first touch of his mouth to hers was terrifying.

'Can you consider it a warning if I say now that we may have to indulge in spontaneous shows of affection if I deem it an opportune moment? I may not have time to ask the question.'

Now Erin was sorry she'd said anything. Next he'd be asking if she wanted to draw up a contract, laying out the terms and conditions for these public displays of affection.

She still wouldn't look at him. 'It's fine. Forget I said anything. I just wasn't expecting it…'

'Erin, look at me. Please.'

Reluctantly she did so, vaguely aware that a charity auction was starting. She resolutely didn't look at Ajax's mouth.

'You're right. I shouldn't have just assumed it would be okay to kiss you like that. Please know that I would never want to do anything to make you uncomfortable, so if you'd prefer we didn't touch at all—'

That suggestion sent a shard of panic down to Erin's gut. 'No… Look, I'm overreacting. Forget I said anything. It's fine.' In a bid to defuse the tension she'd created, she asked, 'What's the charity in aid of?'

'It fights against domestic abuse. It's a cause very personal to Leo and Angel.'

Erin looked at him and he said, 'I don't know the details—I don't think anyone does—but I believe that Angel's father was…violent.'

Erin went cold at the thought. 'That's awful.'

Leo and Angel were up on a dais, urging the crowd on to make bigger bids for different lots. There was a lot of raucous cheering and laughter as people vied with each other.

The next lot flashed up on the screen behind Angel and Leo: a romantic dinner for two at one of Athens' most exclusive rooftop restaurants.

To Erin's shock, Ajax put his hand up, and a friendly bidding war broke out between him and a couple of others.

It was soon whittled down to just two, and the price rose and rose beyond anything that might be considered acceptable for a dinner for two. Erin kept waiting for Ajax to bow out—it was getting ridiculous—but he seemed determined. Finally, when the price was eye-wateringly high, the other bidder faded away and Leo Parnassus brought the gavel down on Ajax's bid.

Ajax turned to Erin and took her hand. He lifted it up, gave her a subtle look, as if in question, and she nodded barely perceptibly. Her heart was racing. He pressed a kiss to the back of her hand, causing a flurry of whispers and sighs. More whispers than sighs.

Erin's face burned. Because even though she knew it was all for show, and entirely cynical, the imprint of Ajax's mouth on her hand was like a brand, and she knew that somewhere deep down she wished that this was a real romantic gesture.

So sure your emotions aren't involved? asked a little voice.

That incendiary thought made her pull her hand free. She didn't look at Ajax—she didn't want to see his expression.

The auction had ended and the crowd were milling around again.

Erin thought of something. 'I got the signed contract back.'

Ajax looked at her. 'I have signed over full custody to you.'

'I saw that.'

Erin felt only a flat kind of acceptance. It would have been strange if he'd had a sudden change of heart, and the last thing she or Ashling needed was someone not being consistent. But still… It was confirmation of his intention to have very little to do with his daughter.

Erin reminded herself that it was absolutely necessary to set out these boundaries. Her own mother had used to just appear at random times and stay for a day or two, making Erin hope and wish that she was coming back for good, only to disappear again. As she'd grown older she'd refused to see her mother on those visits, needing to protect herself from the inevitable disappointment and her resentment at being squeezed into the space between two conferences when she happened to be in town.

Erin said now, 'It can be renegotiated at a later stage if you want to make any changes. Maybe when she's older you'll feel differently.'

Someone jostled Erin from behind and she fell forward into Ajax's chest. He caught her to him with his hands on her bare arms. They were pressed together, chest to chest. She could feel his heart. Or was it hers, pounding too hard?

He looked down at her, and for a moment she thought he was going to kiss her again, but he said, 'I won't want to make any changes.'

The haze of desire in Erin's head cleared. She pulled back, steadied herself, and for the rest of the evening kept a rictus smile on her face. Thankfully Ajax kept their physical contact to a minimum from then on, just hand-holding or lightly touching her back.

She had to nip this seed of hope in the bud. The seed of hope that somehow he'd change and realise that of *course* he wanted a meaningful relationship with his daughter. She'd learnt a harsh lesson from her mother, and she couldn't afford to forget it now.

A few days later, Ajax was looking out through the window of his home office. Laid out before him was the back garden, with Athens in the distance. But he could only see the little tableau unfolding on the lawn.

Erin, Damia and Ashling and much excitement. Ashling had just taken her first steps. Erin appeared to be crying and video calling someone—Ajax guessed it had to be her father—and Damia was holding Ashling. She let her go and the little girl wobbled on two sturdy legs towards her mother as Erin filmed her. Then Erin threw the phone down and caught Ashling to her, standing up and twirling her high in the air.

Ajax could hear their shrieks of delight from here. But it was as if there was a block of ice in his chest. Numbing him. Keeping him safe. At a remove. Memories of Theo's first steps threatened to surface, but Ajax pushed them ruthlessly down.

The pane of glass between him and them was more than a physical thing. Every self-preserving instinct inside him told him to stay far away from this moment, even as another part of him ached to see it.

He could feel his skin getting clammy and his heart starting to pound erratically. Nausea climbed up from his gut. He turned away and walked blindly out of his office and out of the villa, his heart rate only returning to normal as he got further and further away.

It was early evening, and Erin was standing in front of the mirror again, with Georgiana behind her. She felt completely intimidated by what she was wearing.

'Isn't this a little...too much?'

Georgiana stood back and looked at Erin, almost comically insulted. 'Do you have *any* idea where you are going for dinner? Do you know how impossible it is to get a booking? You have to book years in advance!'

Erin said, 'I feel naked.'

'You look *amazing*.'

Erin found it hard to believe. She was wearing a jumpsuit—dark brown-silk, long harem-style trousers. So far, so respectable. But the top was merely two pieces of fabric, slashed almost to the navel, held up by a clasp behind her neck, leaving her back bare.

Her hair was slicked back. Her eyes looked even bigger than usual, shimmering with gold. A gold bangle encircling one upper arm and chunky gold earrings were the only adornments. She wore gold high-heel sandals.

Georgiana said, 'It's daring, chic and elegant. Every man within a ten-mile radius will want you.'

Erin smiled weakly. One thing was sure: she was making up for all those times she'd stayed in studying when her college mates had been out partying.

There was a knock on the door and Erin's heart nearly jumped out of her chest. Surely Ajax would take one look and be horrified? He didn't strike her as the kind of guy who went out with women who were practically naked from the waist up.

She turned around slowly and steeled herself, barely aware of Georgiana slinking away. There was silence. Ominous. Thick with a tension that Erin remembered from before...in that elevator.

She risked a glance at Ajax, and gulped. His eyes were wide and he was looking her up and down. Her skin tingled. She felt sure he had to be horrified.

He was wearing a black shirt and black trousers. Thick hair swept back. She was glad he wasn't in a tuxedo—she couldn't handle that again.

Erin finally blurted out, 'It's too much, isn't it? I'll change... Georgiana tried a dress before this. I can put that on.'

She'd turned, as if to go back to the dressing room, but Ajax said roughly, 'No, it's fine. You're fine.'

Erin turned around again. 'Are you sure?'

A muscle ticked in his jaw. 'Absolutely. We should go.'

In the back of the car as they drove into Athens, to try and defuse the thick tension in the air, Erin said, 'Ashling started walking just the other day.'

'I know. I saw it.'

'You did?' She was surprised.

He nodded. 'From my office.'

'You should have come out. She was so excited.'

Ajax looked straight ahead, as much to avoid looking at Erin in that provocative outfit as to hide his reaction to that image of watching Ashling walk. He felt a familiar tightening in his chest.

'I couldn't. I had to go into the office.'

Erin sat back. He could almost feel her deflation.

'Wow…' she said eventually. 'You really are determined not to get involved at all.'

He looked at her. 'I told you I'm not doing that again.'

She needed to understand, so that she didn't hope he could be more.

Her golden-brown eyes narrowed on him. 'Have you ever considered that your reaction could be due to some kind of trauma, brought on by the death of Theo? Like PTSD?'

Ajax knew what that was. He had a good friend who'd been a French Legionnaire and he'd suffered with it. His friend had even opened a clinic to help others. But Ajax had never considered that the death of his child could have brought on something similar. And yet Erin's words resonated somewhere inside him. Touched on a raw place.

Luckily the driver was pulling up outside the restaurant now, and he took advantage of the distraction to avoid answering Erin's unwelcome perceptiveness.

He went around the car to help her out, taking her hand, noting the apprehension in her expression as she stepped out and straightened up. It was a novelty to be with a woman who wasn't used to this world under the glare of the cameras…a hundred of which seemed to go off as they rounded the vehicle and approached the door which led to an elevator that would take them to the rooftop.

Erin's hand tightened in Ajax's and he put an arm around her waist, tugging her into his side. She fitted against him so easily. Security men opened the door and they slipped inside, where a concierge called for the elevator.

Ajax noticed that Erin was trembling slightly. He looked down. She was pale. He cursed softly in Greek.

'I'm sorry,' he said. 'I should have warned you. I'm so used to the paparazzi being everywhere that it doesn't occur to me that you're not.'

Erin was mortified that she was so shaken, but the barrage of lights exploding in their faces had felt almost like a physical assault. How did anyone get used to that level of aggressive interest?

She moved out of Ajax's embrace. 'I'm sorry. I'm fine. I just wasn't expecting it. I didn't even see them.'

'Don't be sorry—it's not your fault. You're reacting as any sane and normal person would.'

Erin sneaked a glance up at him. His jaw was hard. She had an almost irresistible urge to touch him there, get him to soften. As a girlfriend or lover might. But she wasn't either. She curled her hand into a fist just as the elevator arrived.

It was dark inside, with walls covered in murals. It took Erin a second to realise that they were all tiny depictions of people in various sexual poses. She blushed and looked away—only to find her own image sent back to her by the mirrors, fragmented and disjointed. The curve of a shoulder...her bare back...the curve of her buttocks under the silk. There was a scent like leather and wood. Decadent...

To her relief, the doors opened again and she saw a man waiting to escort them through an archway of thick foliage into the restaurant. Ajax put his hand on her elbow. Erin noted that they hadn't even checked who Ajax was—they *knew*.

As did everyone in the restaurant, it seemed, as heads swivelled when they walked past and conversations stopped.

The restaurant itself was enough of a conversation-stopper. At the top of one of Athens' highest buildings, it commanded views over the city taking in everything from the Acropolis all the way down to the port of Piraeus, gateway to the islands.

They were led to a table with arguably the best views, secluded from most of the other diners by lush potted plants. Candles flickered on the table laid with white linen and crystal glasses and gold cutlery. The air was warm and balmy.

Erin's phone vibrated in her clutch and she took it out to see a message from Damia and a picture of Ashling asleep.

All well here. Enjoy dinner!

From the other side of the table Ajax asked, 'Everything okay?'

Erin smiled. 'Fine. Just Damia sending me a picture of Ashling sleeping.'

She almost moved to show it to Ajax, but after that terse exchange in the car she put her phone away, ignoring the pang near her heart.

The waiter arrived with two glasses of champagne. 'Compliments of the manager.'

Erin smiled her thanks and took a small sip. She looked out over the view. 'It's beautiful up here.'

Ajax was unfolding his napkin, looking down.

Erin protested. 'You're not even looking.'

His head came up and his eyes met hers. 'I'm looking.'

Heat curled through Erin's blood. She had to be imagining the intensity in Ajax's gaze. It was so dimly lit up here... He looked away and Erin breathed in.

'You're right—there's a lot I don't notice, that I take for granted.'

'I guess that's not hard to understand when you grew up in a such rarefied world.'

'I can't deny that. I was born into privilege.'

Erin leaned forward, putting her chin on her hand. 'And yet you're not spoiled.'

Ajax frowned and took a sip of wine. 'That's a good thing?'

She nodded. 'You're not entitled or rude or lazy. You don't have to work, but you do. You don't live a life of empty sybaritic pleasure like a lot of rich people.'

He put his glass down. 'Careful or I might think you actually like me.'

Erin blinked. 'I don't *not* like you. We were...intimate. That wouldn't have happened if I hadn't liked you.'

She suddenly realised the truth of that. The fact that he'd impressed her on lots of levels from the moment she'd seen him. His work ethic. The way he treated people.

She shook her head. 'Why aren't you a spoiled playboy, travelling around the Mediterranean on a yacht?'

He made a face. 'I can't say it ever appealed to me. The thing that was paramount in our family was the respect our name held and the family business. We didn't have time to rebel or zone out.'

The waiter came back and took their orders. Ajax recommended certain Greek specialities to Erin and she happily complied, eager to explore the cuisine.

When the waiter was gone, she said, 'You said you and your brother weren't encouraged to be close?'

A shadow passed over his face for a moment before he responded, 'Yes and no. We were pitted against each other. He was always going to be the first to inherit control of the family business, but I was encouraged to compete with him, as if to keep him on his toes.'

'It's a pity that you weren't just allowed to be brothers.'

'Yes, it is. I did love him…but I felt I never really knew him.'

Their starters arrived—a courgette, peach and sea urchin salad. Erin said, a little regretfully, 'It looks almost too good to eat…'

But then she speared some peach and closed her eyes in appreciation.

When she opened them again Ajax was watching her. Not eating. Erin put down her fork and wiped her mouth with the napkin. 'I'm sorry. I'm probably not meant to really eat it, am I?'

Ajax grinned, and it took Erin's breath away. He looked younger…carefree.

He speared some sea urchin and salad and said, 'Here's to actually eating food!' And he popped the laden fork in his mouth.

Erin felt lightness bubble up inside her as she took some more of the exquisite salad herself.

It was only after the starter was cleared that she had the

nerve to ask a question that had been going around in her head for days.

'Were you ever going to marry and have a family? Or was that just expected of your brother?'

CHAPTER SEVEN

AJAX SAT BACK, his fingers on the stem of his wine glass. He seemed relaxed, but Erin felt the sudden tension. Cursing herself inwardly, she said, 'It's a personal question. You don't have to—'

But he put up a hand. 'You first. What were your plans?'

Erin hadn't been expecting that, but it was only fair. 'All I knew was that I didn't want to be like my father... abandoned and sad. I mean, I was abandoned too, but it was different for me. A parent is one thing...but a partner, a lover... That was devastating for him. He never met anyone else. He was a single parent. It was lonely. I always wanted siblings. But I think I put off thinking about it until I had Ashling, and now I have to think about it.'

'You want a family? For Ashling not to be an only child?' Ajax stated this almost as if it was something outrageous.

Erin looked at him. 'I do. I'd like brothers and sisters for her. And I'd like to meet someone I can spend my life with... I don't want Ashling to be lonely, or to see me be lonely.'

'You surely don't believe in love?' He sounded faintly mocking.

Erin avoided his eye. 'I'm not that naive. In some ways I

think perhaps there is some merit in arranged marriages… partnerships.'

So why did that feel like a lie even as she said it?

'You're a good mother.'

Erin risked a glance at him. 'Apart from the fact that I took so long to tell you about your daughter?'

Ajax shook his head and sat forward. 'You were right, I'm not that accessible, and I know how consuming pregnancy and a new baby is. Even though Sofia had an army of nannies on standby from before the baby was even born, she wasn't immune to the stress and change it brought into her life.'

'Did she want to be a mother?'

'It was more that she was *expected* to have an heir. I don't think she and my brother had quite factored in the speed with which she got pregnant, though,' Ajax said. 'Women don't *mother* in our world,' he added. 'They delegate to others.'

Erin smiled wanly. 'We aren't all that different, give or take a few hundred million euros and a dynasty spanning generations.'

The main course arrived, and Erin was surprised. She was genuinely enjoying talking to Ajax. Even about prickly things.

The main course was sea bream with sautéed seafood, house special mayonnaise and baby potatoes roasted in herbs. The food almost distracted Erin enough not to pursue her questioning—but not quite.

She took a sip of wine. 'So now it's your turn. Were you ever planning on marrying and having a family?'

When Erin had looked Ajax up online, after they'd had their brief affair, nothing salacious had come up before his marriage to Sofia. There were pictures of him with stunning women, but no one had appeared with him more than once or twice.

Ajax sat back. 'I can't say that I'd given it much thought. My brother was already on his way to creating the next generation. If I was to have had a family it would have been purely strategic—to get ahead in the business. There were several women from prominent families who would have been suitable, but now, in restructuring the family business, I've ensured that we're no longer dependent on something as archaic as marriage to foster security or longevity.'

Erin recalled that the future of the company would now be made secure through an independent board of management, under Ajax's control, well out of the hands of family.

'Why was it so important for you to change things?' she asked.

'Because my brother and I had been used as pawns all our lives, purely to carry on the Nikolau legacy. When he died, and I was all but forced into marriage with Sofia to avoid a scandal, I realised just how toxic it was. But really it was Theo who made me see things differently. He reminded me of when I was young and used to see other parents and families…they looked happy in a way I couldn't understand. I didn't want him to have the kind of life I had, brought up and moulded into a good servant of the business and family. He was his own person, and I was determined I wasn't going to force him into anything.'

Erin was touched. 'I think he would have appreciated that.'

Ajax shrugged. 'My grand revelation didn't matter in the end.'

'You changed things anyway,' Erin pointed out. 'You could have left it alone. You could even have walked away.'

Their plates were cleared. Erin declined coffee, but she

was told she had to try the baklava—a Middle-Eastern staple and speciality of the restaurant. As expected, it was delicious. Creamy and sweet, encased in delicate filo pastry that melted on her tongue.

'Amazing!'

She put her spoon down and looked up to see Ajax watching her. Immediately her heart sped up. She really wished she could be immune, so they could navigate this temporary faux romance and move on to the time when he would stay on the very periphery of their lives. All she could hope for was that maybe in time he would come to realise what a mistake he was making in choosing not to parent his daughter.

'Ready to go?' he asked.

Erin nodded, suddenly aware that a lot of the people around them had left.

Ajax let her precede him, then put a solicitous hand on her lower back—which would have been fine if her back hadn't been bare. She could feel his fingers against her skin and they burned.

The manager bade them goodnight and waited by the open elevator doors. They stepped in. Was it Erin's imagination or had the space got smaller? Darker...more decadent? The images of couples cavorting in X-rated poses, small enough to trick the eye but impossible not to notice once you knew what they were, seemed to mock her.

The doors closed, encasing them in the dark, moody atmosphere. The elevator slowly moved downwards. Ajax stood on the other side, back against the wall, hands in his pockets. Supremely relaxed. And yet he had the air of an animal about to pounce.

Or was Erin losing it completely after champagne and a little wine? Quite possibly...

'I really enjoyed that dinner. It was delicious… A little overpriced, considering what you paid at the auction, but—'

'Erin.'

She stopped babbling. Ajax took his hand out of his pocket and came towards her, reaching behind her to press a button. The elevator came to a stop. She looked up at him, her mouth going dry.

She moistened her lips. 'What are you doing?'

'Do you have any idea what you've been doing to me all evening in that outfit?'

Erin shook her head, mesmerised by the look on Ajax's face.

'Driving me insane.' He looked down at her chest. 'All I could think about was sliding my hand under your top and touching you. Feeling the weight of your breast…your nipple growing hard.'

As if on command, Erin's nipples tightened against the material of her jumpsuit. Her breathing was shallow. 'I thought… I didn't think you wanted me like that…'

His gaze moved back up. It was like a beam of heat leaving her skin.

'I haven't stopped wanting you since we were together. I told you that.'

Erin swallowed. 'But that was before you knew…'

He shook his head. 'I still want you. I want to touch you right now. Kiss you.'

Erin had an overwhelming sense of déjà vu…back to another elevator on another continent. But that had been then and this was now. And he still wanted her. And she wanted him. And whatever else was going on suddenly seemed inconsequential.

But a small, sane part of her tried to resist. 'There's no one here to see.'

'I don't want anyone to see.'

Ajax's voice was a throaty growl that resonated deep inside Erin. All the way down to the pulse between her legs, hectically throbbing. Her resistance melted like snow on a hot stone.

'I want you too.'

Ajax moved closer and put his hands either side of her head, on the wall behind her. She could see, out of the corner of her eye, their reflections. His tall, muscular body covering hers.

But then her focus narrowed down to Ajax's mouth as his head lowered and came closer. It covered hers so gently that she wondered if she was imagining it. She reached up and twined her arms around his neck. Suddenly he pressed closer, and the gentle touch turned into something much harder and more incendiary.

Her mouth opened under his, inviting him in, stoking the flames. One of his hands went to her head—she could feel her hair being mussed up—and his other hand splayed across her bare back, before moving around, fingers trailing across her skin, until he found the opening at the front of her top. His hand slipped inside and cupped her breast, thumb flicking against her pebbled nipple.

Erin almost lost the use of her legs, and she had to lock her knees. Ajax tore his mouth away. They were both breathing heavily. She could feel his erection against her lower belly. Hard.

Ajax pulled back a little and, leaving his lower body pressed against hers, used both his hands to push aside the flimsy silk covering her breasts. He looked down and Erin's gaze followed his. He cupped her breasts in his hands, the darkness of his skin making her own look even more pale.

Her nipples stood out, tight and pink, as if begging for

his touch. He bent his head and encircled one straining tip in exquisite heat, sucking and laving it with his tongue.

Erin's fingers speared his hair, holding his head. She writhed against him, unconsciously seeking more. Seeking for him to fill the aching centre of her body.

A voice broke through the heat haze in her brain. It took her a second to figure out that someone was speaking in Greek through the intercom. Erin tugged Ajax's head back up and almost slid to the floor. His eyes were heavy-lidded, dark blue with desire, his cheeks slashed with colour.

At that moment he registered the voice too and stood upright, pulling Erin's clothes back into place. She was shaking.

Ajax said something rapid in response to the voice. He looked at Erin.

She caught a glimpse of her reflection in one of the mirrors and let out a squeak. Her hair was on end and her top was askew, showing half a breast. She smoothed her hair and adjusted her clothes.

Ajax said in a rough voice, 'Ready?'

Erin nodded. She couldn't trust herself to speak. He took her hand and pushed a button. The elevator resumed its progress downwards. The doors opened and Erin couldn't look the doorman in the eye.

Luckily Ajax's car was right outside and she all but dived into the back seat, face burning with a mixture of shame, embarrassment, and also a very illicit excitement. This man brought out a side of her that had never existed before. Not even at college.

The car journey back to the villa was made in silence, but the air was thick enough to cut with a knife. Ajax was a couple of feet away from her, but she could still feel his heat. The impressions his hands had left on her skin…her breasts. They still throbbed, the peaks sensitised. Between her legs she felt molten.

Was he just going to walk away and say goodnight? That would be the wise thing to do. Not to relive the past. So if he did she wouldn't betray how much she wanted him.

But when the car pulled to a stop outside the main door Ajax came and held out a hand to help her out. He didn't let go. They went inside. Wordlessly, he led her upstairs. They stopped outside Erin's bedroom and he said, 'Do you want to check her?'

The implication was clear. It wasn't over.

Erin nodded. She slipped inside and stood at Ashling's cot. The little girl was in more or less the same position as when she'd left her. The door to Damia's room was ajar. The baby monitor was on. She took her own anyway, just in case.

She kicked off her sandals and left her clutch behind. She went back to the corridor, where Ajax was waiting. He took her hand again and led her down to his room. Closing the door behind them.

Erin put the baby monitor down.

He moved closer and took her arm, removing the bangle. She took off the other jewellery. He led her over to the bed. The room was dimly lit. The French doors were open, allowing a warm breeze to flow through.

Ajax stood in front of her and said, 'I want you, Erin. This isn't over between us.'

She looked at Ajax. 'I'm not sure what "this" is,' she admitted, 'but I want you too.'

He cupped her jaw. 'It'll burn out...we just didn't give it time.'

As if *it* was an entity. Maybe it was. Maybe it would burn

out. For him. Erin couldn't ever imagine not wanting him. But then she was less experienced, and so—

Ajax kissed the swirling thoughts out of her head, pulling her to him with his two big hands on her waist. Then he moved them over her back. He opened the clasp at the back of her neck.

The top of the jumpsuit fell away, exposing her breasts. Ajax looked at her, eyes hot. She couldn't wait. She reached for his shirt and undid it, pulling it open, over his shoulders, down and off. She undid his trousers, pulled down his zip, the backs of her fingers brushing against his body and making him suck in a breath.

She stopped, looked up.

He replaced her hands with his and quickly stripped until he was naked. Then he found the clasp at the side of her jumpsuit and opened it, pulling down the zip. The rest of the jumpsuit fell down to the floor and she stepped out of it, wearing nothing but her underwear.

'Get on the bed. I've waited for this for so long.'

That admission landed somewhere that made her feel a little vulnerable, so she shut it out and focused on the physical. Her skin felt hot and tight. She did as he asked, lying back, looking up at him. He was magnificent. All hard muscle and sinew. A smattering of dark hair across his chest. Narrow waist.

He put on protection and then pushed her legs apart. He said, 'I need this—*you*—now. Okay?'

Erin nodded wordlessly, humbled by the evidence of his attraction to her. How had she not seen it?

He lodged his body in between her legs and took her in one smooth, cataclysmic thrust. She was ready for him, but she still gasped at the sensation of his body joining hers, stealing every last breath and any rational thought. She also—dangerously—felt emotional. She hadn't thought she'd experience this again with him.

He moved, slowly, torturously, in and out, letting their bodies get reacquainted, but it wasn't long before need gripped them both and their movements became more and more urgent, frenzied.

They reached their peak at the same time, both bodies taut, pressed against each other, before spiralling down and down into the never-ending waves of pleasure.

Ajax's body was heavy over Erin's for a long moment. She revelled in it, holding him to her as the breeze whispered over their sweat-slicked skin. And before she could stop it the ebbing waves of pleasure were pulling her down into a deep state of relaxation.

She didn't notice when Ajax pulled free of her body and went to the bathroom, nor, when he came back and got back into the bed beside her, pulling the sheet over them and curling himself around her body.

When Ajax woke he was alone in the bed. Dawn had broken. It was the second time Erin had left the bed before he'd woken, making him feel exposed. Discombobulated. On all counts where this woman was concerned nothing had ever gone to plan.

Like his intention to keep the boundaries between them in spite of his desire. But last night...in that flimsy, silky jumpsuit...the boundaries had been burnt to ash. He'd almost taken her in that elevator. The second time he hadn't been able to control himself in a confined space with her.

Clearly there was unfinished business between them, and he wouldn't feel a sense of control again until whatever this was between them had burnt itself out. If he hadn't let her go when he had, nearly two years ago, maybe he would have known about her pregnancy at the start and things would be very different now.

How, exactly? asked a sly voice.

Ajax ignored it. He got out of bed and showered and dressed.

He heard the sound of the baby's babbling before he saw her. He felt a clutch of his gut, the urge to turn around and go in the opposite direction, but something made him stop. And go towards her.

Erin and Damia and Ashling—in a highchair—were on the terrace, having breakfast. They all looked at him, and Ajax fought down the prickling feeling of panic and exposure.

He met Erin's eyes. As before, when they'd slept together that first time, she looked composed and as if nothing had happened. Her hair was still damp from showering. She looked fresh in a sleeveless top that turned out to be a sundress, he saw, when she stood up momentarily to pick up the spoon Ashling had dropped to the ground.

The housekeeper came out with coffee for Ajax. He sat down. Damia excused herself and left them alone. Ajax willed Erin to look at him, but she was fussing with Ashling, who was looking at him with big eyes—brown and green, like her mother's. Other than that, she'd inherited his colouring. Thick dark hair and dark golden skin.

It was the first time he'd really taken her in, and something about that shamed him now.

As if sensing his focus on her, the baby held out the spoon she'd just dropped. Ajax knew he was on shaky ground, and that if he stayed here, engaged with her, he would be blasting apart the walls that had protected him for the last few years.

He was taking a risk. But he couldn't look away from her.

In spite of the fear, he put out a hand. 'For me?'

Ashling smiled. Something turned over in Ajax's chest. He took it. 'Thank you.'

She smiled again, showing glimpses of emerging teeth. When he glanced at Erin she was looking at him warily. But then she schooled her expression and went back to feeding the baby what looked like a mixture of yoghurt and fruit.

'You were up early,' he said.

A little colour washed into her cheeks. 'I didn't want the baby to wake you.'

'Her name is Ashling,' Ajax pointed out, with not a little irony.

Ashling reacted. *'Abba!'*

'I don't think it was a good idea…last night,' Erin said in a low voice, as if he might not know what she meant.

Everything in Ajax rejected that. 'I think it was inevitable.'

She shook her head. 'We shouldn't…again.'

'No one is forcing you into anything, Erin.' He watched more colour flood her cheeks. Good. Maybe she was remembering that she'd been with him every step of the way last night.

She looked at him. 'It's not that I don't want to…it's just not a good idea.'

'Probably not,' agreed Ajax. 'But I think it's obvious that it won't be finished until we've let it run its course.'

She wiped Ashling's mouth and looked at him, 'You make it sound like a virus.'

It *was* a kind of virus—in his blood. A hot and urgent virus. And it was the same for her and they both knew it.

Damia came back out and took Ashling to get washed and changed. The baby looked at Ajax over Damia's shoulder as they went out, her gaze seeming far too old for her age. As if she knew the turmoil she caused inside him.

'We're going into Athens to go sightseeing today,' said Erin. 'It's a bit cooler with the clouds.'

Ajax looked back at her. *'We?'*

'Me and Damia and Ashling.'

'I'll arrange for you to have a driver.'

Erin protested. 'We can get a taxi or use public transport.'

Ajax shook his head. 'Non-negotiable.'

Erin looked as if she wanted to argue, but eventually she said, 'Okay—fine.'

Ajax got up and went over to where Erin sat. He put his hands on the arms of the chair either side of her. He saw how her pupils enlarged and the colour in her cheeks grew more hectic. His blood hummed.

'I enjoyed last night.'

She looked up at him. He could see the resistance in her expression, in her eyes. She wanted to lie. To refute it. But she couldn't.

She seemed to sag a little. 'So did I.'

He stood up and couldn't stop a smile.

She scowled at him. 'Is that it?'

He put out his hands. 'Are you trying to invite me to make love to you here on this terrace, right now?'

He turned and walked away, chuckling, and then felt something hit him between his shoulder blades. He turned around. It was a small *pain au chocolat*.

Ajax picked it up and backed away, still facing Erin. He took a bite and exclaimed with relish, 'Almost as delicious as—'

She threw another pastry at him and Ajax let out a laugh.

It only occurred to him as he was driving to the office in Athens that he couldn't remember the last time he'd felt so light.

* * *

Later that day Erin and Damia were wilting in the heat. They'd stopped to sit outside a café in the shade. Ashling was in her buggy, with a muslin cloth shading her and a fan blowing cool moist air over her sleeping form.

Erin loved how child-and-baby-orientated the Greeks were, fussing over Ashling everywhere they went. It seemed to be so at odds with what Ajax had said about his family—but then they weren't exactly mere mortals.

Erin smiled at Damia. 'Thank you for being tour guide today. You were fantastic and your English is superb.'

The young woman blushed and smiled. '*Efharisto*, Erin. And your Greek is really coming on.'

Erin lifted her glass of chilled water in salute. She was doing her best to pick up some Greek, feeling that it was only respectful to do so.

Damia's gaze went to something behind Erin just as the back of her neck prickled with awareness.

Ajax appeared at her elbow.

She knew it was him before she saw him.

'Good afternoon, ladies, I trust you've had a good time?'

Erin smiled up at him, hating the way her body went into roadrunner mode, her pulse skyrocketing. 'Lovely, thank you. Athens is an amazing city.'

'Well,' he said, 'if it's all right with you, Damia, I'd like to steal Erin away.'

Immediately Erin protested. 'That's not fair. She's been out with me all day—she shouldn't have to work into the evening too.'

Now Damia protested. 'It wasn't work, really, and of course I don't mind. Do you want me to take Ashling home? It's almost time for her supper anyway.'

Erin felt a little redundant. After a year of being a single parent, suddenly she wasn't alone any more.

Reluctantly, she said, 'If you're sure you don't mind?'

Damia shook her head. 'Not at all.'

Ajax said, 'Damia has agreed to come back to the island with us when we go tomorrow. She'll work with us for the duration of your visit.'

Erin looked at the young woman, 'Can you do that?'

'I have the summer off to work and learn English, and working for you ticks both those boxes. Plus, I'll get to visit my great-aunt.'

It was all working out so seamlessly Erin felt suspicious—but she wasn't even sure of what she should be suspicious. This was a world where things appeared as if by magic and there were no obstacles.

Damia stood up and gathered up their things. The driver parked nearby and Erin lifted Ashling out of the buggy. She was a heavy weight, still dead to the world.

She woke up briefly when she was installed in the baby seat at the back of the car, but after a sleepy smile at Erin fell asleep again. Erin gave instructions to Damia, told her to call her if Ashling wasn't settling, and then they drove off.

'She'll be fine with Damia,' Ajax said.

Erin felt prickly and disgruntled, and all for no reason she could put her finger on. It was this man...inserting himself under her skin.

'I'm just not used to this level of support.'

'You'll have this level of support whenever you want it now. Money isn't an object.'

Erin rolled her eyes. But she still found it intimidating,

Ajax's level of wealth. 'It's not all about the money. I don't mind caring for my daughter.'

'If you go back to work full-time you'll need a nanny.'

Erin stopped. She hadn't even realised that they were walking away from the café. Ajax must have paid their bill.

She looked at him. *Work*... She hadn't even thought about work. She was in danger of forgetting an outside world existed.

That revelation didn't help her prickliness subside.

She thought of what he'd said about working full-time. 'I never mentioned going back to work full-time. Not explicitly.'

Ajax shrugged. He was wearing sunglasses. Together with chinos and a dark blue short-sleeved polo shirt he looked like a movie star.

'I just assumed. You're good at your job.'

They continued walking. The early-evening air was still balmy. Erin just wore a light top tied around her waist over the sundress, and her cross-body bag. She resembled every other tourist there. The prickliness faded. She realised in that moment that she felt more carefree than she could recall feeling in some time. If ever.

It was an unwelcome revelation when she was with someone who didn't inspire feelings of carelessness or freedom. But since she'd noticed that little moment at breakfast, when Ajax had interacted with Ashling, albeit briefly, it had felt as if there'd been a subtle change in the air. Signifying what, exactly, Erin didn't know—and she wasn't sure if she wanted to know. For some reason she didn't want to dwell on it, sensing some kind of danger.

She diverted her mind back to what Ajax had said. *'You're good at your job.'*

She stopped walking again. 'I am good at my job.'

'You are.'

But something was striking her now. She continued walking and said, 'You know… I just automatically pursued the career that I had the most aptitude for without ever really stopping to think about it. My parents are both academics, and the standards they set were high, but they never put pressure on me. It was all my own pressure.'

'Are you saying you don't really want to be an attorney?'

Erin's stomach lurched at that audacious idea, but she felt something like a fizzing excitement. 'I don't know… I know that I'm not missing my job as much as I thought I might. And I know that working full-time and leaving Ashling with nannies is not something I want.'

'You can do whatever you want, Erin. You're qualified to choose from a myriad of roles.'

She hadn't thought about it like that before. And she certainly wouldn't have had Ajax Nikolau down as a careers advisor. But since he'd told her about the expectations his family had put on him and his brother she was realising that her experience hadn't been that dissimilar.

Ajax came to a stop outside a boutique. In the window mannequins were dressed in jewel-coloured gowns.

Erin quipped, 'Not quite your colours, but I'm sure you'd look great in them.'

'Ha-ha.' Ajax took her elbow in his hand. 'Not for me—for you.'

Erin resisted. 'But Georgiana has brought more clothes than I could wear in a lifetime.'

'Indulge me,' Ajax said. 'There's an event next week, hosted by my family, and it will require something…specific.'

'What kind of event?'

'An annual family gathering.'

Erin could feel her blood drain south. 'Is it a good idea for me to meet them?'

'You're the mother of my child,' Ajax pointed out.

'A child you don't intend having much to do with.'

Ajax's jaw clenched. 'Maybe I'm rethinking that.'

Alarm bells rang. 'What's that supposed to mean?'

He ran a hand through his hair. He obviously really didn't like being questioned. Well, tough. He couldn't flip-flop like this about something as important as his daughter.

'Something you said about Theo's death having a profound impact on me... It made me think. I realised that my motivations in staying out of Ashling's life are based on fear. Blind, irrational fear. And that's not good enough. For me or her. Or you. You both deserve more.'

Erin was speechless. She knew she should be welcoming this development but for some reason she felt unsettled. Maybe because she didn't trust that he meant it? Or thought that he would change his mind? She was only protecting her daughter after all.

Ajax arched a dark brow over his glasses. 'I thought you'd be happy.'

Erin flushed. 'Of course I am. But if you make any connection with her now it will cause upset if you can't continue.'

'I'm aware of that. That's the last thing I want to do.'

Erin knew instinctively that he would be a good father. His devotion to his nephew told her that. So why wasn't she more happy about this change of heart?

'Shall we?' Ajax indicated the boutique.

She'd forgotten about it. Up to now Ajax hadn't wanted

to be involved and Erin had resigned herself to getting on with their lives without him. But now she felt as if she was on shifting sands, and suddenly she wasn't sure where they were headed any more.

CHAPTER EIGHT

Ajax HAD GIVEN instructions to the boutique owner and, after taking Erin's measurements, she'd gone to pull out a selection of clothes.

'What's wrong with the clothes Georgiana has brought?'

Ajax made a face. 'Nothing at all— for an Athens crowd. But I just want to make sure you feel comfortable. My family are conservative. And snobs.'

'That sounds ominous.'

'Think of it as a kind of armour.'

'Wow…now I really can't wait to meet them.'

The owner came back and indicated for Erin to come into the changing room. She left Ajax outside.

The clothes that the woman had chosen—far from the classic Chanel-type suits Erin had been envisaging—were relaxed. Elegant and not a million miles from what she would have chosen herself. There were trouser suits with pencil trousers and structured jackets. Dresses in every colour of the rainbow, long and flowy, that swirled around Erin's body. Beautifully cut jeans and soft cashmere tops. Silk shirts…

And then the evening wear.

Erin tried on a dress that she could appreciate might fit a more conservative environment than a restaurant or his friends' charity auction, but to her it seemed even more daring than anything Georgiana had picked out.

It was made of a green silk that made her hair look even redder than usual. It had spaghetti straps and a piece of fabric that covered her breasts, with cut-outs at her waist. The dress then fell in soft, Grecian-style folds to the floor.

Erin said, 'Um… I'm not sure about this one—'

She stopped when a movement caught her eye, and looked up to see that Ajax had pulled aside the curtain to look. She could feel the heat in his gaze from a couple of feet away and quivered inwardly, remembering how it had felt to have his body surge into hers the previous night, stealing her soul piece by piece.

'We'll take it,' said Ajax. 'And the rest.'

Ajax pulled a pair of jeans and a silk top out of the pile of clothes, and a pair of high-heeled sandals.

'Put these on for now.'

Erin knew she should protest, but she was ashamed to admit that having Ajax telling her what to put on, dressing for him, gave her a bit of a thrill. She put on the clothes and the boutique owner told her that everything else would be packed and sent to the villa.

Erin sighed. She'd have to try and remember this wasn't how things worked in the real world.

When she'd changed, they walked outside and found Ajax's car waiting. They got into the back and it moved into the traffic.

'Where are we going?' she asked.

'Just a little taverna I know.'

Just a little taverna turned out to be an exclusive restaurant, tucked away in a picturesque square in the ancient Plaka area. It was full already, with a mix of tourists and glamorous locals. Erin was in awe of the Greek women, blinging with jewellery and stunningly beautiful.

A table was found for them in a discreet corner. When they'd sat down, Erin said, 'More opportunities for us to be seen out and about?'

Ajax shook his head. 'No, actually. I'm hungry and thought you might be too. There are no paparazzi here.'

Erin's insides dipped. Was this a date?

'So what is this? What are we now? Friends?'

With benefits? She didn't say that.

Ajax's mouth quirked. 'You know, that's one of the things I like most about you—your directness.'

Erin wasn't sure if that was a compliment. She could imagine other women being more coquettish. It just wasn't her style.

'I could say the same of you.'

She shivered a little at the memory of how 'direct' Ajax had been that first night. In the elevator

'We're lovers,' Ajax said then. 'Lovers for as long as this mutual attraction lasts.'

Erin wanted to ask, *How long?* But a waiter arrived and took their order, brought water and wine.

Erin took a sip of the chilled white wine. 'What if one of us loses interest first?' She knew it wouldn't be her, as humiliating as that was to admit.

Ajax shrugged. 'Let's cross that bridge when we come to it.'

'Our contract will have to be drawn up again, to reflect your desire to have a relationship with Ashling.'

'We're in no rush. I trust you.'

Erin absorbed that. It was huge. She literally had a contract signed by them both, stating that he was giving her full custody. She could go back to the States with Ashling and refuse him access. He'd have to take her to court to renegotiate.

But of course she wouldn't do that.

As if reading her mind, Ajax said, 'I know you wouldn't use that against me.'

'No,' she admitted, 'because I've worked for you, and all I can say is I'm glad I was on your side.'

Ajax widened his eyes. 'I'm a pussycat.'

Erin snorted. 'You're a shark.'

He smiled, showing his teeth, but all that did for Erin was remind her of how he'd nipped at her bare skin in intimate places. She squirmed on the chair, glad he couldn't see into her mind, which seemed to be stuck on one track: *Ajax*.

After revealing that he wanted to have Ashling in his life, Erin felt newly exposed. As if a layer of protection had been taken away. That was something she couldn't unpick now. Not while Ajax was looking at her.

'So, both your parents are still alive?' she asked.

Ajax nodded. 'My father handed over the reins of the business to my brother, and then to me when Demetriou died. Essentially, he's retired now.'

Erin was curious. 'He wasn't that passionate about the family business, then?'

Ajax's mouth flattened for a moment with distaste. 'The only thing he's passionate about is whoever his current mistress is. All very discreet, of course. She won't be at the family gathering.'

'You don't approve?'

'It's disrespectful. He was the one who had affairs first, and I could see what it did to my mother, even though she'd deny it to her death. It made her vulnerable. Brittle. It pushed her further from us, her sons, because her life became all about competing with my father to try and make sure he knew she wasn't hurt.'

'But it sounds like she *was* hurt,' Erin observed. 'Maybe there were feelings there after all.'

Ajax didn't respond to that.

Erin couldn't help asking, 'Did Sofia have affairs...?'

'Yes. Of course. We didn't share a bed.'

'Oh.' Erin hated how that made her feel lighter. 'But surely you weren't going to live your life celibate?'

'To be honest, I was consumed with Theo. I didn't think too much beyond him for the first couple of years. Sofia and I had already made an agreement that after a respectable amount of time we'd quietly divorce, and I would get full custody of Theo.'

'She was willing to hand him over?' Erin knew she shouldn't be shocked after her own experience.

Ajax shrugged. 'I told you—women in my family don't really do mothering well. They're not expected to.'

'I know not everyone automatically feels that rush of love—for some parents it can be incredibly complicated—but *you* felt it...and you weren't even Theo's biological father.'

Erin was surprised when a waiter appeared to clear their plates—she hadn't even noticed that they'd been served starters and had eaten them. Ajax seemed to have an effect on her that meant she was in some sort of bubble, where the world didn't impinge. Dangerous. Seductive.

She'd had to be responsible for so long, due to her father's scattiness, that she'd never really had the luxury of taking her foot off the pedal. But here in Greece she felt as if she was having the first holiday of her life.

Albeit along with the rollercoaster effect of Ajax on her body, mind and emotions.

No, refuted a voice. *Not emotions.*

It was just physical. As he'd said, it would burn out— even if it felt as if it was burning brighter and hotter now than it had even on that first night.

When they'd returned to the villa, Ajax stopped beside Erin, outside her bedroom door. They looked at each other. Her heart thumped. The air crackled between them with unspoken desire. She went inside, checked on Ashling— who was asleep, with Damia's door open nearby—and then went back out to Ajax, who was waiting.

He held out a hand. Erin took it, even as she felt, super-stitiously, that some line she couldn't see was being crossed.

In Ajax's room they were naked and on his bed in seconds. Ajax's big body was moving over hers with such mastery that Erin could only hope he wouldn't see how he triggered her emotions. She couldn't deny it here…naked. She could only ride the wave and pray that when she was washed up on the shore again she would still be in one piece.

When Ajax woke the following morning it was early. The bed was empty beside him, but he wasn't surprised now— even if he didn't like it.

And since when had he wanted to wake up with a woman?

Since Erin.

He scowled. His body was heavy with sensual satisfaction, and yet he could already feel the edge of hunger forming again, just thinking of the previous night and how he'd felt he would die if he didn't sink into Erin's tight, slick embrace before taking another breath.

It would burn out.

It had to.

And yet even as Ajax automatically formed that thought, a part of him was asking, *what if it doesn't?*

He didn't dwell on that ridiculous notion—because desire always burnt out.

He got up and showered and dressed, then left his room, stopping by Erin's bedroom door.

He pushed it open and saw that she was in bed, on her back, in a T-shirt. Even seeing her clothed turned the spark into a flame deep in his belly.

Not burning out yet.

She was fast asleep.

He heard a sound and looked towards the open door leading into the nursery. Even though he felt the urge to turn and walk away, not to engage, he went into the room.

Ashling was standing in the cot, hands on the bar, gabbling to herself, quite content. Then she saw him, and for a second Ajax held his breath, expecting her to cry. After all, he'd barely engaged with her at all.

But she didn't cry. She smiled. And Ajax's chest swelled so much he couldn't breathe. Somehow he found his way to breathing again and his feet took him over to the cot.

Ashling immediately held up her arms. Ajax lifted her and closed his eyes against the wave of déjà vu.

He'd told himself he would never feel this again...the soft, heavy weight of a child. But here he was.

Ashling looked up at him and said something unintelligible. Ajax knew that there was no going back from this moment.

Just then, a sleepy Damia appeared in the doorway, tying a robe around herself. She said, 'I'm so sorry, Mr Nikolau. I didn't hear her.'

He shook his head. 'She wasn't crying. It's fine. I've got this—you go back to bed and get some sleep.'

'Are you sure?'

He nodded and she left, closing the door. A familiar pungent smell hit Ajax's nostrils. He wrinkled his nose and looked at his daughter. 'Ah, yes…the not so pleasant bits of parenting… Let's see if I can remember what to do, hmm?'

Ashling just looked at him with a wisdom beyond her years, as if to say, *I'll indulge you for now, but don't push it*, and Ajax pressed a kiss to her head, silently praying that he could cope with the fear and hope that it didn't consume him.

When Erin woke she was disorientated. Alone in her bed. Then it came back in a rush. The urgency that had gripped her and Ajax. The aftermath when she'd felt torn apart but also more whole than she'd ever felt.

That was what had spurred her to leave his bed as he'd slept. She'd checked on Ashling, showered, and then crawled into her own bed. And now… She squinted a look out through the windows and sat up in a panic. Now the sun was high.

She jumped out of bed and went straight into the nursery, to find it empty. Damia must have taken Ashling down for breakfast.

Erin quickly washed and changed into denim shorts and a loose shirt. Barefoot, she went downstairs and followed the sounds of Ashling's babbles, a deeper voice, and Damia's laughter.

Not sure what to expect, she walked out onto the terrace to see Ajax with a napkin over his face, playing peekaboo with Ashling, who was in the highchair. The detritus of breakfast, bits of food and a spoon, were all over the ground in the vicinity.

Ashling was squealing with delight every time Ajax's

face was revealed. Erin could empathise, she thought, but there was something about the tableau that unsettled her.

Like a coward, she shied away from investigating why this evidence of Ajax playing with his daughter wasn't causing her to feel any sense of happiness. She almost felt... scared. She told herself it was because she feared Ashling would get hurt. Every moment with Ajax like this now had the potential to cause damage when he inevitably got bored or changed his mind.

He's not your mother, whispered a voice.

Ashling spotted her and immediately held out her arms, saying, 'Mama-mama-mama.'

Erin scooped her up, feeling almost guilty to be breaking up her moment with Ajax. Ashling snuggled into her.

Ajax stood up. He was wearing a suit—dark grey—a white shirt and a tie. Erin spotted a blob of something and pointed. 'I think you have some baby food on your jacket.'

Erin waited to see how he'd react, but he was sanguine. He got a napkin and dampened it with water and dabbed at the mark. Another tick in his favour. But consistency would be key.

He looked at Erin and she fought not to blush as she sat down and poured herself a coffee, holding Ashling in one arm.

He said, 'I'm going to the office for a couple of hours. I'll meet you and Damia and Ashling at the airfield. My assistant will come and help you pack, and the driver will bring you to meet me.'

Erin glanced up. 'Okay, we'll be ready.'

When Ajax had walked away, with Ashling looking after him over Erin's shoulder, Erin said to Damia, 'Thanks for getting her up this morning. I didn't hear a thing.'

Damia said brightly, 'Neither did I! It was Mr Nikolau.

He changed her and dressed her and brought her down for breakfast.' Damia stood up. 'I'll clear up and then go and get ready. Just shout if you need me for anything.'

The girl walked away, towards the kitchen, and Erin sat there, stupefied. Ajax had got Ashling up and changed her nappy. Not an especially remarkable thing at all—especially for a father. But for a man who just a little more than twenty-four hours ago had been intending on staying out of his daughter's life it was not just stepping over a boundary—it was smashing it aside and setting it on fire.

Erin forced herself to calm down. This was a good thing. He was obviously familiar with babies after Theo. Changing a nappy wasn't a big deal for him, evidently. He'd confided in her that he'd intended on getting full custody of Theo. He'd obviously been very hands-on.

She assured herself again that this was a good thing. A positive development. So why did she feel so uneasy?

Agatha welcomed them back to the villa with open arms. Damia was clearly delighted to see her great-aunt, and conversed with her in rapid Greek for a few minutes, with Agatha making dramatic exclamations in response.

Erin was surprised and a little disconcerted at how much it felt like coming home.

Agatha and Damia swept into the house, taking Ashling with them before she could even protest. Ajax took Erin's hand and led her straight upstairs to his bedroom, closing the door.

'Ajax, we can't... We just got here... I need to change Ashling and give her something to eat.'

'Agatha and Damia are fighting over her right now.'

Erin's back was to the door. Ajax put his hands by her head, caging her in. She could easily duck down and slip away but, fatally, she didn't want to. She couldn't help revelling in Ajax's hungry gaze. He'd shown her a sensual side of herself she might never have explored with anyone else.

Never would again.

Her heart hitched.

She tipped up her chin. 'Well, then, what do you propose we do?'

'One thing I've wanted to do with you but haven't yet… because each time I wake up you're gone.'

He'd noticed she was gone. And he didn't look all that happy about it. Something flip-flopped inside her.

'What's that?' she asked.

'Take a shower together.'

Erin nearly melted into a puddle at his feet, but she managed to say nonchalantly, 'I do feel a bit…dusty.'

Ajax reached for her hand and led her into the bathroom, 'Well, then, let me help you feel less…dusty…'

Erin followed him on jelly legs, giving up any attempt to rationalise what was going on.

The sun beat against Erin's closed eyelids. She could hear the sound of crashing waves. The air was scented with sea and sand and earth. Her body felt heavy and deliciously replete.

They'd had lunch at the villa not long ago, and afterwards Ajax had taken Erin and Ashling off to explore the island, bringing them to this secluded beach that was totally empty.

Erin was momentarily out of the shade, trying to get her skin to warm up to a shade of golden brown that she'd never attained before. She could hear splashes and squeals of delight, and she came up on one elbow and put her shades on. She couldn't quite believe what she was seeing. Ajax, in snug swim-shorts, in the shallows of the sea, held Ashling in his arms, ducking her down into a wave as it crashed around them.

She was loving it. She'd never been to the sea before. She was covered in factor fifty—as was Erin—and she was wearing an adorable flowery onesie and a sun hat.

Ajax's volte face with his daughter still unsettled Erin. She felt sure that this was just a phase, perhaps brought on by memories of Theo. Once they returned to the States and Manhattan, and the realities of co-parenting sank in, they'd see less and less of Ajax.

Erin bit her lip. She should be protecting Ashling now, from inevitable disappointment, but maybe she was young enough that when Ajax gradually disappeared she might not be devastated.

Erin had little doubt that this was how it would play out, because the alternative was something she couldn't even grasp. The thought of Ajax being part of Ashling's life but not Erin's…of him moving on and marrying…as she might do herself some day. Blended families? He didn't strike her as the kind of guy who would put up with that, so he would just excise Ashling from his life.

But the image in front of her now mocked that assertion. Father and daughter, playing in the surf, Ashling clinging on to Ajax like a monkey.

In the last couple of days he'd become her new favourite person. His ease with her and his tactility was unbelievably impressive, and seductive in a way that impacted on Erin deeply.

He beguiled everyone—even babies. When he looked at you, it was like the sun shining all around you.

It was what would happen when that sunbeam moved elsewhere that Erin needed to be ready for.

As if hearing her thoughts, Ajax turned around with Ashling and looked at her. The sea water was sluicing off his tall, broad body. Ashling put out a pudgy hand and gabbled something that sounded like *'Mama...mama...'*

Erin levered herself up from the sand and walked down the beach towards them, very conscious of the green one-piece swimsuit she'd chosen. It was perfectly conservative, but under his devouring gaze it felt positively indecent.

Something was happening here that Erin hadn't expected. A family was forming, in spite of every instinct screaming at her that it couldn't possibly be real.

And yet as she neared Ajax and Ashling in the sea, and they both reached out for her, she told herself not to trust in the shimmering possibility that this might exist. This was fleeting and temporary. All of it. She couldn't afford to forget that.

'I feel a little overdressed for the village.'

Ajax slid her a look from the driver's seat. 'You look perfect.'

He was taking her to a local restaurant for dinner. She was wearing a dress that Damia had picked out. A cream silk sleeveless wrap dress that fell to her feet. She tucked a wayward lock of hair behind one ear.

'Your hair is getting longer.' Ajax observed.

Erin made a face, 'I cut it because Ashling kept grabbing it when she was a tiny baby, and because —'

She stopped suddenly. She hadn't been intending on elaborating.

But of course Ajax had noticed.

'And because...?'

Reluctantly she divulged, 'Because it reminded me of my mother. Her hair was long...and I used to be fascinated by it. One of my earliest memories is of lying in bed and wrapping it around my hand. Maybe even then I knew she was going to leave.'

'So you cut it for practicality, but also maybe to send a message that you weren't going anywhere?'

Erin looked at him. She wanted to scowl. Ajax was far too perceptive sometimes. 'I hadn't thought about it like that.'

Ajax parked the car on a quiet street and they got out. The evening air was warm and balmy. The sun had set, leaving the sky pink and rusty and golden.

They walked down a cobbled street towards the water. The houses were white and blue, with colourful flowers blooming from pots and planters. Children were running in and out of houses, squealing with excitement.

Erin couldn't help smiling at their effervescence. It made her yearn a little for Ashling to have this kind of experience... But the reality was that Erin probably wouldn't be here to witness it. Ashling would be coming to spend time with her father on her own. Perhaps with half-siblings. Erin couldn't help but think that Ajax might now be more open to children, marrying again...

She was lost in that train of thought when Ajax, beside her, said, 'Look up.'

Erin lifted her head and gasped. They were at a small marina, with the sea lapping against the wall just in front of them. Boats bobbed gently on the water. Restaurants were spread out on each side, buzzing with locals and tourists. Candles and fairy-lights added to the atmosphere. Soft music came from the tavernas. Handsome waiters lured prospective diners into their establishments.

Ajax led her to the left-hand side, to a taverna at the very end. The owner welcomed Ajax like an old friend and gave them a table right by the water's edge.

'This is…stunning,' said Erin. 'I've never been anywhere like it.'

'You haven't been to Europe before?'

Erin wrinkled her nose. 'Only the main attractions like London and Paris on school or university tours. I was too busy studying and then working. During my summers I'd work to make money.'

'Even though your mother was giving you an allowance?'

Erin could appreciate now how she'd shut off a vital part of her youth in a bid to show her independence. Her work ethic.

She looked at Ajax. 'It's a bit pathetic and boring, isn't it?'

He shook his head. 'I never did the travelling thing either. I've just travelled a lot with work. I think I'd prefer to come somewhere like this for the first time at the age of twenty-eight and really appreciate it, rather than see it on a whistlestop tour at eighteen and forget it.'

Erin looked out at the sea. There were fishing boats in the distance with their lights on. The moon was rising. She said, 'You could never forget this.'

The waiter came, with Greek wine and food. It was rustic and delicious. Fish so fresh Erin could taste the sea.

She sat back when their plates were cleared, refusing dessert. 'I couldn't eat another bite. That was…amazing.'

Ajax couldn't take his eyes off Erin. She eclipsed the view. She wore practically no make-up, but her eyes were huge and her mouth an enticement to kiss her until she was breathless, arching her body into him in a way that blew his mind.

Her skin was turning a very delicate shade of golden. Freckles had appeared on her shoulders and nose. Traces of her Celtic heritage. Her hair *was* getting longer, softening around her face. His gaze drifted down, taking advantage of her looking out to sea. Her arms were slim, but strong. Hands elegant…short nails, no varnish. No frills, no fuss. Straightforward. And yet he sensed hidden things…depths that he didn't yet know.

Usually at this point with a lover Ajax veered instinctively away from wanting to delve into anything personal. But this woman… She still intrigued him, and he wanted to know more.

He looked back up and saw there was a small smile playing around her mouth. Ridiculously he felt piqued.

'What's so amusing?' he asked.

She looked at him and he felt the impact of that golden and green gaze in his solar plexus. And lower. He shifted in the seat, cursing his lack of control.

She lifted her hand, put her forefinger and thumb about an inch apart, and whispered, 'I think I'm a little bit drunk.'

Ajax grinned. She'd had a little more wine than usual, and he'd had less as he was driving. She seemed looser… less vigilant. She looked altogether too seductive to resist— and he had no intention of doing so.

He stood up and put out his hand. 'Come on, let's go home.'

To his surprise a shadow crossed her face, and she suddenly looked a lot less loose. But then, as if he'd imagined it, she put her hand in his and let him pull her up.

They walked back up to the car and he couldn't help asking, 'What was that back there?'

'What?'

'Your reaction to what I said...*let's go home.*'

There was something there. Ajax could sense it.

But Erin shook her head. 'Nothing at all.'

She wouldn't meet his eye, though, and for the first time since he'd known her he suspected she was lying.

When they got back to the villa, Erin moved down through the garden towards the pool.

Ajax stopped. 'Where are you going?'

She turned around, but kept walking backwards. 'For a swim.'

Ajax shook his head and followed her through the gap in the bushes. The pool was visible under the moonlight, but Ajax went and turned on the low pool lights.

Erin pointed. 'This is the deep end, right?'

'Yes...' Ajax said, wondering what she was thinking.

But before he could wonder for too long she'd kicked off her sandals, stepped up to the side and executed a graceful dive into the water, fully clothed.

She swam underwater the entire length of the pool, a shimmering elongated shape, before emerging at the other end. She stood up and pushed back her hair with both hands.

Ajax nearly lost control of his legs and had to lock his knees. The water had made her dress completely translucent. He could see the curves of her breasts and the pebbling of her nipples. And down between her legs he could see the darker shadow of the hair that covered her sex, where he imagined her slick and ready.

He dragged his gaze back up. She was just looking at him.

For some reason he felt it was important to resist the almost overwhelming urge to join her. 'Why do I have the feeling that you're trying to distract me?' he asked.

She arched a brow. 'Because you have a suspicious mind?'
That was it.

Ajax's control dissolved in a rush of lust.

He pulled and tore off as many clothes as he could and dived into the water, barely making a ripple. He swam to Erin's legs, under the water, and put his hands around her calves, tugging her under.

They looked at one another under the water, the world blocked out. Ajax had the impression that she was a siren, a mermaid, and that he would never really know her.

He put his mouth over hers and she wrapped her arms around him. There was something fierce about the urgency that gripped them as he surged up out of the water with her. They gasped for air.

He pulled her dress apart and it came away from her body. He threw it to the side. Her bra was transparent. He didn't even bother taking it off. He cupped a breast and covered the pouting flesh with his mouth, sucking and nipping at her, making the nipple harder.

He was barely aware of her breathless entreaties and moans. He reached under the water and pulled her underwear down. And his own. He lifted her and instructed her roughly to wrap her legs around his waist.

She did. She lay back against the side of the pool, the water lapping around her.

Ajax's body was so hard it hurt, but he delayed the gratification, spreading his hand up over her belly to her breasts, exploring the plump flesh, and then moving up higher, tracing the elegant line of her neck and jaw.

Her eyes were huge, bright with desire. 'Please, Ajax...'

He looked at her. In this moment everything was stripped away. He still didn't know her secrets—but he would.

He hitched her a little higher and then with one movement entered her slick body. She threw her head back, the sinews in her neck standing out.

He moved in and out slowly, and then gathered pace, driving into her body harder, faster. She lifted her head. She was biting her lip and Ajax covered her mouth with his, just as the storm gripped her and her inner muscles clamped down so hard on his body that he couldn't breathe for a second.

He exploded deep inside her, felt her muscles gripping him and milking him of everything. Every last piece of strength.

In the aftermath, as the world returned around them and the laboured sounds of their breathing diminished, Ajax was aware of something niggling at the edge of his mind. Something urgent. But he couldn't focus on it.

He pulled free of Erin's body and levered himself out of the pool with effort. He reached down and helped her out, trying not to let her body enflame him again.

He took her hand and led her over to the changing area, fetching a couple of robes. He helped her put one on. Her eyes were half closed and she looked flushed and languorous. He belted the robe tightly around her waist, as if that might help him maintain control.

He put on his own robe and, after gathering up their discarded clothes, took Erin's hand again to lead her up to the villa.

Halfway across the lawn, though, she stopped and took her hand away from his. He looked at her and saw she was pale. She looked back at him and said, 'Protection. We didn't use anything.'

Immediately the niggling sensation stopped. That was what it had been. And for a man who would usually have been zealous about protection, he found to his surprise that the thought wasn't causing him a sense of panic.

Erin's expression *was* reflecting panic, though. But then it cleared a little and she said, 'Actually, I think it's okay. I'm at a safe place in my cycle.'

Ajax didn't want to decipher why he wasn't feeling more relieved. 'That's good… I'm sorry, that was my fault. I should've stopped.'

CHAPTER NINE

ERIN'S HEART WAS still pounding after what had just happened, and also with the gut-churning panic of realising they'd made love without protection. But she was pretty sure it would be okay...

Ajax's face was hard to read in the moonlight, but Erin had the distinct impression that he wasn't overly perturbed about the fact that they'd just had unprotected sex.

She winced inwardly. Not that having protected sex had been all that effective twenty-one months ago.

Her body was still tingling all over. She couldn't quite believe she'd had the audacity to jump into the pool with her clothes on, and then what had ensued...

But he'd been right—she had been trying to distract him. From how it had made her feel to hear him say so casually *'let's go home'* after dinner.

Let's go home.

As if they were a regular couple on a date night. Enjoying some alone time away from their baby and then returning to their home.

Their home.

When it wasn't remotely her home. It was Ajax's home. And yet in that unguarded moment she'd desperately wanted it to be her home too. *Their home.* The kind of place where there were two parents and one of them didn't just get up and walk out one day, leaving a trail of destruction in their wake.

The fact that he'd exposed that deep-seated desire had made her feel very vulnerable. Vulnerable to the possibility that she might even be hoping for something more than she'd ever dreamed of.

So she'd acted on instinct. And diving into the pool had almost been as much about waking herself up out of that dream as anything else. But then Ajax had joined her...and madness had taken over, scrambling her mind and making her forget that she needed to stay vigilant and not be dreaming of impossible things.

Erin took a step backwards now. 'I should go and check on Ashling...go to bed... Goodnight, Ajax.'

She turned to walk away and reassured herself that any day now the heat in Ajax's gaze would fade, this insane interlude would end, and they'd go back to New York and—

'Would it really be so bad?'

Erin stopped. She didn't turn around. She was afraid she was having some sort of aural hallucination—that Ajax had probably said goodnight, but she'd heard something else. Something ridiculous.

She turned around. Ajax's face was still in shadow. Not helping.

She said, 'What did you say?'

He stepped forward and into the soft light coming from the villa. He should have looked ridiculous in the short towelling robe, but he didn't. He looked sexy.

He said, 'Would it be so bad if you were pregnant?'

It took a moment for that to really compute in Erin's brain. For her to try and interpret the dozens of threads that question contained, all leading in directions that had alarm bells screaming.

'Of course it would—what are you talking about?'

Ajax took another step forward, closing the distance between them. There was an intent look on his face. Erin's sense of extreme vulnerability came back.

He said, 'Think about it. We already have a child. We have amazing chemistry. We like each other. You and Ashling are making me think about family again, even though I swore I wouldn't.'

We like each other.

A tepid emotion, at best. Not the kind of emotion that could sustain a long life, build a family.

You need love for that.

Erin clamped down on that rogue thought. She didn't want love. But she wanted more than just 'like',

She shook her head. 'You said yourself this chemistry won't last. Only days ago you were still determined not to have anything much to do with your daughter. And have you forgotten that you dumped me?'

Ajax's face tightened. 'I never forgot you.'

'I had no idea you were still thinking about me.'

'I came back for you.'

Erin all but rolled her eyes, the memory of him dumping her and the hurt and humiliation still vivid. 'It sounds like you expected me to be waiting for you, frozen in time from the last moment we'd seen each other.'

A muscle ticked in his jaw. 'I admit I handled it badly. I wanted you too much. You got too close, It freaked me out. I shouldn't have let you go.'

'And yet you did.'

But the sense of betrayal suddenly felt less. Ajax's admission that he'd made a mistake settled deep inside her, where she didn't want his words to land. They were too easy.

Too seductive.

She waved a hand. 'Look, the past is the past. We are where we are. We have a child, and what we're doing is protecting her future. The fact that you want to be involved is very welcome, but I don't want a family with you, Ajax.'

'You want a family with someone else?' He said this flatly. 'You'd prefer that our daughter would be brought up by someone who isn't her father? For her to have half-siblings?'

'There's nothing wrong with that. Many families—'

'I know.' Ajax cut her off. 'I'm not saying there's anything wrong with it—if that's how it happens organically. But I think we have something we can build on. Some marriages are made on a lot less than that—you said so yourself.'

Had she? This was different, though. She felt confused. Her priority was to protect Ashling from harm. From being rejected or abandoned by her father. Yet now Ajax was asking her to consider having more children—which, as far as Erin could see, would only multiply that threat.

She imagined a scenario where she *was* pregnant again and what if Ajax changed his mind? Or maybe realised that the trauma of losing Theo was too big to surpass and he retreated back out of their lives again?

His change of heart was still too recent, too sudden to trust. That's what she told herself now.

Erin shook her head. 'No, I don't think it's a good idea.'

'I'm offering marriage, Erin.'

'Is this a proposal?'

That muscle moved in his jaw again. 'Not the most romantic, maybe, but yes.'

At this evidence that he would actually be willing to marry her for every reason except for love, or romance, Erin had a seismic realisation. The realisation that she *did* want love, even though it scared the life out of her. She knew now that it was the only thing that would sustain a happy life. And maybe she'd find it someday with someone, but not with Ajax.

She said, 'This isn't about romance or love, I know that. But if my parents had had love—mutual love—then maybe my mother wouldn't have left. Because she would have loved my dad enough to stay. Loved me enough at least to try.'

For a second—a heart-stopping moment—she wasn't sure how Ajax would respond, and the sense of being on the edge of a cliff about to step into the void was dizzying.

Then he said, 'I can't offer you love, but I can promise to be faithful and supportive. To respect you.'

Erin's dizziness faded. Of course he didn't love her. And she didn't love him. She didn't want him to love her.

She shrugged. 'Then I think I'll be a better parent to Ashling living authentically, rather than turning our fake relationship into a fake marriage and bringing more children into the mix. That's not the antidote to how I grew up—it's just another form of dysfunction.' Before he could say anything else, and confuse her, Erin went on, 'You can't admit that your parents' example of an arranged marriage was any better? We'd be somewhere halfway between that and what I had. And,' she said, 'I don't think we should do this again.'

'Do what again?' Ajax asked, civilly enough, but she could hear the steel in his voice.

'This...' Heat came into her face. 'Sex.'

The air seemed to throb with the tension between them.

Eventually Ajax said 'So what, you're saying you want more now? A real relationship? Love?'

'Maybe…would that be so bad?'

'I've told you I can't offer that.'

'I know.' Erin felt hollow.

At Ajax's stony expression she said, 'Maybe we should just go back to New York?'

But he shook his head, 'What about the event with my family? They should meet Ashling, at least.'

She wondered why, after everything she'd just said, she was feeling a sense of relief that he wasn't agreeing to put her on the next plane out of Greece.

He said, 'The event is this weekend. We'll be travelling to another island not far from here for a couple of nights. In the meantime I'll have my PR team assess the situation in New York—and, yes, I think you should be able to go back to New York after that.'

Erin looked at him. 'I think that would be for the best. And then we can establish a routine that suits Ashling.'

Everything in Ajax was rejecting Erin's, oh, so cool reaction to his proposal. He—Ajax Nikolau—had just *proposed*! But he realised in that moment how arrogant he had been to assume Erin would be impressed enough to collapse at his feet in a heap of acquiescence.

This was Erin. Had he learnt nothing?

But as for her assertion that they wouldn't have sex again…

The thought made him feel feral. Dangerously unmoored.

How could she stand there and say that when the flush of their lovemaking was still on her skin? After that…

conflagration? This woman uniquely had the ability to turn him from civility to primal instinctiveness within seconds.

She'd talked about love. Of course he didn't love her. Theo's death had almost destroyed him. He knew that if anything happened to Ashling it would destroy him all over again, but all he could do now was put blind faith in the universe not to be so cruel for a second time.

But as for Erin... The thought of allowing himself to feel for her what had almost destroyed him...

No. His blood went cold at the thought.

Erin was looking at him, waiting for a response. He could deal with everything else she'd said in time, but as for *no sex*...

He walked closer to her. Close enough to touch. He saw how her eyes widened and flared. The way the pulse beat hectically at her throat.

He said, as coolly as her, 'I know this proposal has come as a bit of a surprise, and I wasn't expecting to talk about this here...now... But I would just ask that you think it all over before making a final decision.'

Her jaw was tight. 'Okay. Fine.'

Quickly, before she left, he said, 'As for the other thing... not making love again... I've never forced a woman in my life and I'm not about to start. But if you think this is over between us, then you will have to prove you have the control to resist it.'

She went red in the face. Ajax imagined that if steam could come out of her ears it would. With that, he sauntered away and into the villa, leaving her standing there.

But it was a pyrrhic victory, because he was very much afraid that she would prove to have far more control than him.

* * *

A few days later, Erin was still stewing over Ajax's parting bombshell after that cataclysmic moment in the pool. He'd all but dared her...told her that she couldn't possibly hold out against him.

Luckily, she hadn't been tested. Since that night he'd spent most of his time in his office, working, and had appeared only briefly for meals, or to play with Ashling—who was now his biggest fan.

Seeing her bonding with her father made Erin both delighted and terrified at once. Because with every day that their bond deepened and became stronger the stakes were rising. And if he ever walked away from Ashling...

And the proposal. Had that really happened? Or had she dreamed it? In any case, it hadn't been a proposal—not in any romantic sense. It had been a proposition: *We get on, we have a kid, we should get married*.

The thought of agreeing to marry Ajax and living a life where the desire between them gradually fizzled out to be replaced with companionship... if they would even have that...sent shudders through Erin. She'd been fooling herself to think she could live with a scenario like that and it was beyond ironic that Ajax was the one who had made her realise she wanted more.

Ashling squealed from somewhere behind her on the small plane that was taking them to Ajax's family event on another island. An island owned by the family.

She looked behind her, and against every instinct she melted inside. Ashling was on Ajax's lap. He was trying to read some paperwork, and she kept trying to grab it. He put it down and lifted Ashling to face him. She put her hands on his face.

Erin felt a very inappropriate twinge of envy.

She got up and walked down the plane. Ajax looked up. Erin felt the effect in her blood.

She put out her arms. 'I'll take her—you're working.'

Ajax lifted her towards Erin and for a second their hands met as she took Ashling. Erin had to grit her jaw against the spark. *No.*

Ajax said, 'We'll be landing shortly anyway.'

Erin sat down on a nearby seat, suddenly trepidatious. 'So, who is going to be there?'

'My parents. Aunts, uncles, cousins. Some of Sofia's family.' Ajax's mouth thinned. 'After all, that's why my brother was going to marry her. Her family are also one of the oldest and most prominent in Greece.'

'It must be hard for them…losing her and Theo.'

Ajax made a rude sound. 'Not that you'd know it. Our marriage united the families and that's all they care about.'

'They sound truly…inhuman.'

Ajax shrugged. 'It's just a different world for them. It's how they've been brought up.'

Erin hugged Ashling a little closer.

Ajax saw the movement and said, 'It's exactly what I don't want.'

He looked at her then. Explicitly. The offer was still there.

Before he could see how he affected her, Erin fled back to her seat and occupied herself with Ashling for the rest of the flight.

It was a small, pretty island, with a bustling harbour town, iconic white and blue houses all along the sea front. They were driving up over the hill behind the harbour, towards a massive villa in the distance, surrounded by lush greenery.

Erin had noticed at least a dozen private jets parked up

at the island's airport. Nerves churned in her belly. She was definitely out of her comfort zone now. She recalled what those people in Athens had said about her: *ambulance chaser*. She smiled a little grimly at herself. They'd also said Ajax would never want to marry her, but they'd been wrong about that.

If she wanted it…but she didn't.

She'd asked Georgiana for advice over a video call, and the stylist had helped her pick out some clothes. She was wearing a relaxed light blue suit—culottes and a matching jacket—with a cream sleeveless silk top underneath. Wedge sandals. A little more make-up than usual to feel fortified. Minimal jewellery.

She'd dressed Ashling in a cute romper suit with a matching sun hat that she kept trying to pull off.

Erin suddenly felt a surge of protectiveness for her daughter, at the thought of bringing her into this lions' den. She wanted to ask Ajax to turn the car around and take them home.

Home.

She had to stop thinking of here as home. New York was home. Where she had her life with Ashling.

They were at the villa now, and pulling into a huge courtyard. Uniformed staff hurried out to greet them. Damia was in the car behind, and Erin was grateful not only for the help but to have a friendly face.

Erin got out of the car and lifted Ashling out of her seat. The little girl was tired. She hadn't had her morning nap on the plane, too excited by everything, and Erin could sense a cranky storm brewing. She hoped she could put her down soon.

Ajax put a hand lightly on her lower back, but it burned

even through two layers of clothes. He said, 'Might as well get the initial introductions over with.'

He led Erin into the villa—a vast space. Her first impression was that it was cold—which should have been welcome, considering the heat outside. But it was cold in a way that signified little human emotion.

Lots of white pristine surfaces. Expensive art. Furniture that looked as if it had never been touched...

And then a slim, older woman appeared, walking towards them, tall and impossibly elegant, with a cap of silver-grey hair and light eyes. Beautiful but remote. Erin realised this had to be Ajax's mother.

They greeted each other with air-kisses and Ajax said, 'Mother, how nice to see you.'

Erin just watched, wide-eyed at this dry exchange. Even Ashling seemed to have been struck dumb.

The woman turned her gaze to Erin and Ashling. Ajax moved closer, and despite everything Erin was glad of the sense of protection.

He said, 'Mother, I'd like you to meet Erin Murphy and your granddaughter Ashling.'

'Erin, this is my mother Andromeda.'

A fittingly intimidating name. Erin tried to imagine her smiling and saying, *Call me Andi*, and almost wanted to giggle, but she knew it was just a little hysteria.

The woman held out her hand. 'Lovely to meet you, Erin.'

Erin shook her hand. 'You too.'

The woman's light blue gaze went to Ashling. She said, 'So this is the child?'

Ajax's tone was dry. 'Yes, Mother. Your granddaughter.'

'Ashling. Yes, I know. An Irish name. I looked it up.'

Erin tried to hide her surprise.

'She's a pretty thing,' Andromeda said. 'Very like—' But she stopped there abruptly.

She'd obviously been about to say *Theo*. To Erin's further surprise, she thought she saw a flicker of something on Andromeda's face—a flash of emotion. But then it was gone.

She stepped back. 'Your father is out on the terrace.'

They went out there, with Erin letting out a shaky breath. The tension in the air was almost unbearable.

Ajax's father was tall and handsome. Dark eyes. He showed no great interest in Erin or Ashling.

Erin felt Ashling starting to squirm and took the opportunity to excuse herself, fearing a meltdown.

Ajax led them away. As one of the staff showed them up to their rooms he said, 'Well? What do you think?'

Erin had to say, honestly, 'They're pretty much as you described them.'

Except she couldn't forget that little flicker of something on Andromeda's face when she'd almost mentioned Theo. Surely the woman had some humanity in her somewhere?

Erin was shown into a vast bedroom with an en suite bathroom and dressing room. It also led into a room that had been decorated as a pretty nursery.

'Did your parents do this especially?'

Ajax said from behind her, 'No, this was Theo's room.'

She turned around, immediately concerned. 'Is this all right?'

But to her surprise, Ajax looked…okay. Sad, but okay. Erin's heart clenched.

He said, 'I haven't actually been back here since he died. All his things are gone—they did that at least.'

'Ashling can stay in the main room with me. We don't have to use this.'

Ajax shook his head. 'No, it's fine. It's good that it'll be used again.'

He knocked on yet another door and Damia opened it after a few seconds, revealing that she too was just next door.

Ashling clapped her hands and Damia reached for her, saying, 'I'll change her and put her down for a nap.'

'Are you sure?' asked Erin.

Damia nodded. 'Absolutely. That's why I'm here, remember?'

Erin smiled wryly. She still wasn't completely used to having assistance on tap. 'Okay, thanks. But shout if you need me.'

Ajax said, 'I'll show you around and then we'll get a coffee.'

As Erin followed Ajax around the impressive property she had an appreciation of just how vast the Nikolau wealth was. He wore it lightly, so it was easy to forget just how rarefied his world was.

There were numerous gardeners tending to gardens as far as the eye could see. There were several guesthouses. A private stairway led down to a private beach and a jetty where a small yacht was moored.

They stood on the bluff above, with spectacular views out over the sea. The horizon was dotted with other islands.

'Most of the family have their own villas on the island. We'll be hosting some relations and close family friends in the guesthouses, but you probably won't even notice them.'

Erin wrinkled her nose. 'Your family have friends?'

Ajax chuckled. 'In their own dysfunctional way, yes.'

Erin felt warmth spreading through her. It was so easy to be with Ajax like this. Even in the midst of such grandeur and obvious tension. Too easy. Too seductive. She wanted to slip her hand into his and curl closer. Touch him. Use their desire to try and negate his family's chilliness.

But that wasn't her role. And she wasn't going to give him the satisfaction of giving in.

She took a step back. 'Where is the event taking place this evening?'

Ajax looked at her. 'At a rented villa.'

'This one wasn't up to scratch?' Erin quipped.

Ajax shook his head, the corner of his mouth lifting slightly. It made Erin's heart thump. She'd once wondered what it would be like to see this man smile or laugh.

He said, 'Oh, no, this isn't sufficient at all for showcasing the Nikolau dominance.'

Erin loved it that he was able to see his family for what they were. And on that note she took another step back. The word *love* was creeping into her head far too frequently for her liking. It was as if now that she'd given herself permission to desire more for herself, a floodgate had opened. It was just dangerous to conflate *love* and *Ajax* together.

'I think I'll go and get a bite to eat and then give Damia a couple of hours off. She'll be babysitting tonight.'

'I'll come for you when we're leaving...around five.'

Erin nodded. 'I'll be ready.'

Or as ready as she could be. Meeting Ajax's parents hadn't done much to quell her nerves.

CHAPTER TEN

IF ERIN HAD been impressed by his parents' villa, this one was on another level entirely. Apparently it was owned by another Greek billionaire, who was currently renting it out rather than living in it.

It was a soaring, white modern edifice on about three levels. It had been taken over by an events team and decorated with lanterns and fairy-lights. Uniformed staff in black and white moved through the guests—of which Erin counted about two hundred—with trays of sparkling wine and canapés that looked too good to eat. So she didn't. Anyway, she was terrified of getting anything on her evening dress.

She'd thought it was over the top, but Georgiana had convinced her and she was glad she'd listened now because she did blend in. The dress was cream silk with a halter neck design, leaving her back bare, and slashed from her throat to navel where a jewel detail pulled the slinky fabric together before it fell in folds to the ground. She'd teamed it with high-heeled silver sandals.

Damia had helped her with her hair and make-up while Ashling had played with all the new toys that they'd found in the nursery—a nice touch, Erin had thought.

She'd nearly fainted when Ajax had told them they were

taking a helicopter to the other island. Her adrenaline was still pumping and Ajax's hand was on her bare back, which wasn't helping. She would have asked him to remove it, but she remembered that they were supposed to be together.

Maybe she could convince him that now would be an appropriately public time to have a spat. But he was steering her towards people, and she soon got used to nodding and smiling inanely as he introduced her to distant relatives and acquaintances.

Everyone was perfectly civil, but there was a distinct lack of warmth, or fun. And since when had Erin been into *fun*?

Since you started making love with practical strangers in elevators and jumping into swimming pools fully clothed, whispered a sly voice.

She shook her head to get rid of it.

Ajax looked at her during a break in the never-ending stream of people. 'Okay?'

She forced a smile. 'Fine.'

Then she felt Ajax tense beside her. A couple were approaching. Probably in their sixties. Handsome. Not unlike his parents. He greeted them with the same kind of dry air-kiss as he had his mother and then said, 'Erin, I'd like you to meet Sofia's parents—Mr and Mrs Karakis.'

Erin's insides plummeted. She shook their hands, and couldn't help blurting out, 'I'm so sorry for your loss. I can't imagine how devastating it has been for you.'

Sofia's mother looked at Erin as if she had two heads. As if she'd said something completely incomprehensible. Then they moved away again.

Erin felt bewildered. 'What just happened? Should I not have sympathised with them?'

Ajax was shaking his head. 'No—I mean, yes, of course.

Because you are from the normal world, where people experience emotions and are compassionate. But in their world it was a loss, yes, but as you can see it didn't end their world.'

Ajax sounded a little bitter.

'You feel the loss more keenly than they do,' Erin observed. 'Probably for Sofia too.'

'I visit their graves,' Ajax confided. 'Mainly to see Theo, I'll admit, but he's buried with Sofia. There's never any evidence of anyone else visiting.'

'That's really sad.'

At that moment they were interrupted by someone else, and the endless round of introductions started again. At some point the sound of soft jazz music came over the lawn and Erin swayed on the spot. She'd always enjoyed dancing.

As another couple headed their way Ajax took her hand and said, 'Want to dance?'

Erin said gratefully, 'Yes, please—if it means we can avoid more meaningless conversations with people trying to impress you.'

But as soon as Ajax had taken her into his arms on the dance floor, where some other couples were moving in slow circles, she realised her mistake. She was pressed against Ajax, who was obviously taking full advantage of the situation.

She looked up at him and he smiled. It was wicked.

'You were the one who wanted to dance.'

Erin tried to put some distance between them, but it was impossible. So she gave in and let her body do exactly what it wanted: cleave itself to Ajax's like a magnet. The thin material of her dress was no barrier to his body, sheathed in a black tuxedo. She swore she could feel every taut muscle and sinew... And then, when he moved a certain way, one muscle in particular.

She glared at him and he shrugged. 'I can't help it. With other women I can control myself, but not with you.'

The fire in Erin sizzled, as much as she wished it wouldn't. He couldn't control himself around her...?

Almost accusingly, she hissed, 'You said this chemistry would fade.'

'That's been my experience with other women. But you have proved to be unique. It doesn't feel like it's fading to you, does it?'

She could feel the very tantalising evidence of his non-fading desire right now. She shook her head.

'So why deny yourself?' he whispered in her ear, his mouth almost close enough to touch her skin.

Erin tingled all over. Her mind was beginning to get blurry, but she forced herself to stay focused. 'Because, unlike you, I do have self-control.'

She smiled sweetly at him and saw his eyes flash.

This was a dangerous game they were playing, and she knew it. At that moment, though, she caught Andromeda's eye over Ajax's shoulder. She was dancing with her husband, and they couldn't have looked more stiff and unhappy.

She nodded her head slightly at Erin, acknowledging her, and Erin nodded back. But she shivered inwardly—not from desire, this time, but at the reminder of what lay ahead of her if she gave in to Ajax's version of a future for them. A sterile, sad life.

She looked away and forced ice into her veins.

'What's wrong?' Ajax asked.

Erin shook her head. 'Nothing—just someone walking over my grave.'

She somehow managed to get through the rest of the evening, staying as rigid as she could by Ajax's side. And then, mercifully, they were heading back to his parents' villa.

The helicopter landed at a far enough distance from the villa not to disturb Damia and Ashling, and they were driven to the house in two cars. Erin and Ajax in one, his parents in the other.

When they got out at the villa Andromeda was already there. She stopped Erin on the way in, when Ajax was already inside.

Andromeda looked at her and said, 'You're in love with him, aren't you? I saw you dancing. I saw the way you looked at him.'

Erin tried to suck in a breath, but she couldn't. She shook her head, desperately negating the tight feeling in her chest and the pounding of her blood at such an audacious suggestion. 'No, of course I'm not. I know what this is. We both do. It's not love.'

Andromeda smiled faintly, but it wasn't kind. It was sad. 'I'm sure he's told you what it was like for him and his brother. I'd hate for you to get hurt. You seem like a nice woman, Erin. You deserve more.'

Andromeda walked away, leaving Erin reeling, her words revolving sickeningly in her head.

'You're in love with him, aren't you?'

No. She wasn't. She couldn't be. To love a man like Ajax would be the worst form of self-harm. He'd already dumped her once. And while he was offering to spend his life with her, create a family, the offer wasn't born out of love. He might not dump her again, but he would gradually fade away—which would be worse than any kind of abandonment or outright rejection.

Even the prospect of loving Ajax and allowing him that

much power to hurt her, as she'd only been hurt once before in her life—by her mother—made her feel dizzy.

'Erin? Are you okay?'

Ajax. When she least wanted to see him. He was at her side, holding her elbow. He looked angry.

'What did she say to you?'

'N-nothing, honestly. I'm just tired—and hungry, I think. We didn't really eat.'

Ajax took her hand in his before she could stop him, and it was easier to just leave it there. He led her into the kitchen, silent at this hour of the night apart from the humming fridge.

He said, 'Sit down,' and all but pushed her gently into a seat at the table.

Erin sat, and watched, bemused, as Ajax spent an inordinate amount of time opening and closing doors.

Eventually she said, 'What are you looking for?'

He looked at her. 'Eggs.'

She pointed to the pantry door. 'Try in there.'

He did, and said, 'Ah!' and came out with a tray of eggs, triumphant. Erin moved to stand up, but he put up a hand. 'No, stay there. I'm making you something to eat.'

'But you don't know how to cook.'

Ajax looked a little embarrassed, and Erin was gobsmacked to see him efficiently cracking eggs over a bowl.

Eventually he said, 'Since that night when you were in my apartment…'

The second night they'd been together, when they'd skipped dinner and gone into his kitchen at midnight, looking for food. Ajax hadn't had a clue where anything was, but he'd managed to find a chicken salad and some bread. Erin had teased him about his lack of culinary skills.

Ajax continued, 'Something you said stuck with me…

about how could I be self-sufficient if I couldn't even boil an egg?'

Erin winced. Sometimes she was too straight. 'I'm sorry... I didn't mean it as an insult.'

He looked at her over the bowl, where he was now whisking the eggs like a professional. 'No, you did me a huge favour. I taught myself how to boil an egg and then I kept going. I make a mean omelette now. I can't say I've added too much to my repertoire, but I'm hoping to master a decent roast chicken at some point.'

'The easiest thing in the world,' said Erin, trying to ignore the way her insides felt as if they were melting and somersaulting at the same time.

Ajax was now transferring the eggs to a warmed pan and adding in some things she couldn't see. But it smelled delicious. After a few minutes he came over and put a plate down in front of her. A perfectly fluffy omelette, garnished with fresh herbs and some bread.

She looked up at him, mouth agape. And then she shut it again. She was starving. She tasted the omelette and closed her eyes in appreciation.

Ajax poured wine into two glasses and put one down for her. He took another seat.

When she'd swallowed some more food and a sip of wine she said, 'Not hungry?'

His eyes were hooded and the gleam in them was wicked. He said, 'Oh, I am—but not for food.'

Erin refused to let him see how that affected her. Like a match to dry tinder. She was very conscious of her dress and the amount of skin she was showing. She forced herself to finish the omelette and eat some bread, even though her appetite had suddenly diminished.

She took another sip of wine and said, 'That was delicious, thank you. I should go up now…check on Ashling.'

'She's fine. I checked when I came in.'

Another tummy somersault. She ignored it. 'I'm still going to bed.'

She stood up, the silk folds of her dress falling to the floor. She must look ridiculous. Ajax didn't stand up. He sat in a louche sprawl in the chair, his bow tie undone, jacket gone. Stubble on his jaw.

He said, 'You know where I am, Erin.'

She refrained from saying anything and swept out of the kitchen with as much grace as she could muster, all but running to her bedroom as soon as she was out of his eyeline.

She got inside her room and kicked off her sandals, then went silently to the nursery. Her heart expanded when she saw Ashling asleep, lashes long on her cheeks. She pulled up the thin blanket and put her hand on her belly for a minute, feeling the rise and fall of her breath.

Once again she was struck by how protective she felt. She would never do anything to harm this child. In moments like this the betrayal of her mother was as acute as it had been almost twenty-five years ago. She would do anything to spare Ashling the same pain, and if that meant ensuring they kept Ajax at a distance then so be it.

The door to Damia's room was ajar. Erin took the spare baby monitor into her own room and changed into sleeping shorts and a singlet top, washed her face and got into bed.

But an hour later she was still lying there. Wide awake. Restless. Eventually she fell into a fitful sleep and a disturbing dream, in which she was at a party but was encased in ice and couldn't move. No one was looking at her. They couldn't see her. She was trying to grab their attention. And then Ajax was there, but not looking at her. He was with another woman. Erin was sobbing and calling out, begging for him to notice her—

And then she woke up, sitting straight up in bed, heart pounding, skin slick with perspiration. Still that awful icy cold lingered, reaching all the way into her heart.

She didn't think—she acted on instinct. She got out of bed and took the baby monitor with her. She left her room and walked down the corridor to Ajax's room, pushed open the door. He lay in a sprawl on the bed. Naked.

As she approached he woke up and came up on an elbow. His voice was rough. 'Erin...?'

She put down the baby monitor and lifted her arms, taking off the singlet top. She pulled down the shorts and climbed into his bed beside him. He looked stunned. She might have appreciated it more if she hadn't had the overwhelming lingering dread of that dream in her blood.

He touched her jaw. 'Am I dreaming?'

She shook her head. 'No, I'm real. Make love to me, Ajax.'

There was no triumph in his gaze, just pure desire as he pulled her over him and speared his hands in her hair, drawing her face down to his so he could kiss her. She revelled in feeling his body under hers, so strong and warm. His heart beat against hers. Her breasts were crushed to his chest. She opened her legs and he moved her subtly, so she was lined up with where his body was hardening.

There was practically no sound apart from their laboured breathing as he joined their bodies with one thrust. Erin sat back, putting her hands on his chest as she rode him, moving up and down. Ajax put his hands on her hips, holding her as he pumped into her, making her gasp out loud.

The orgasm broke over Erin almost before she had time to register it was coming. Ajax flipped them over, so he was on top, and just before he came he pulled free of Erin's embrace, so she felt the hot warmth of his climax on her belly.

After a few long moments of letting the world come back to its centre, Ajax got up and picked Erin up from the bed as if she weighed no more than a bag of sugar and took her into the shower. Under the hot spray he washed her, and himself, then wrapped them both in towels and took her back to bed, where she finally fell into a dreamless sleep.

When Erin stole out of the bed the next morning, she resolutely refused to look at why she'd gravitated to Ajax so desperately the previous night. Without even thinking about it. Following an instinct she hadn't been able to ignore. For her survival.

She was still wearing the robe he'd put on her after the shower, and she picked up her night clothes and left his room. Back in her own room, after quickly checking Ashling, she had a shower and got dressed.

Ashling was just waking up, and Erin changed her and took her downstairs to give her some breakfast. She noticed that Ajax had washed the plate and pan from the previous night and left them drying on the sideboard. She almost wanted to curse him for being so…unexpected.

She took her and Ashling's breakfast out to the terrace and enjoyed the quiet before others emerged. She would put last night down to an urge to make the most of her chemistry with Ajax before it went away. He was right—why deny themselves? It was just sex.

But what about that dream?

Erin shut it down. The memory of how cold she'd felt was still vivid in the morning light. Of how she'd needed him.

Ashling was cranky, in spite of her good night's sleep, and Erin could see that her cheeks were red. She was teething.

After breakfast, Erin took Ashling down to the beach, to try and distract her, but she was soon working herself up into a state—she'd given her some medication, but it didn't seem to be working.

So Erin brought her back inside to try and find something else to alleviate the pain.

There was no sign of Ajax—which Erin was grateful for. She was sure he'd be mocking and arrogant after her spectacular capitulation last night.

Damia was on the terrace, and offered to take Ashling, but Erin said, 'No, you have the day off. You were working until late and we'll be out again this evening.'

Erin took the baby upstairs. Ashling's wails were now reverberating all through the villa.

To her surprise, Andromeda appeared, holding a teething ring. She said, 'It belonged to Theo. I kept it. Can I try?'

She held out her arms and Erin realised she meant to take Ashling.

Against her better instincts, Erin handed Ashling over, fully prepared for the little girl's wails to increase in crescendo, but to her shock the surprise of being in a stranger's arms silenced Ashling for a moment, and Andromeda put the teething ring against Ashling's lips. She latched on to it immediately, chewing down on it and holding it with both hands.

Andromeda was saying, 'There, there,...that's not so bad, now, is it?'

Erin just gaped at her.

Andromeda looked at her a little sheepishly. 'I could never do this with Demetriou or Ajax. I wasn't encouraged to hold them.'

'I... I heard,' Erin said faintly.

Andromeda jiggled Ashling up and down a little and

walked with her out to the terrace. Then the tiny hairs went up on the back of Erin's neck.

Ajax.

She turned around, saw he was looking past her to his mother. 'Is that…?'

Erin nodded. 'I know… I can't believe it either.'

Then Ajax looked at her. 'You left my bed again.'

Erin pushed aside the way he made her feel…confused and excited and scared all at once.

His expression was stark. He opened his mouth to speak again, but his mother came back with a now much more peaceful Ashling. She handed her to Erin and said, 'I'd like to see her sometimes, if that's possible… I mean, after this is over.'

'Of course,' Erin said, trying to hide her shock, 'you're her grandmother.'

The older woman touched the baby's cheek and then looked at Ajax. With a suspicious brightness in her eyes she said, 'I'm sorry that I wasn't able to be there for you and your brother in a more meaningful way. I wanted to be… But…' She shook her head and left the small room quickly, before Ajax could respond.

He looked at Erin, stunned. 'Did you see that?'

Erin nodded. She felt a little sad. 'I think she's realising, since losing your brother and your nephew, that maybe she's been given a second chance. It's a good thing, Ajax.'

'If she means what she says,' he said tautly.

Erin appreciated the irony that Ajax now felt the same fears she had regarding him.

'Maybe you should go and talk to your mother. I'm going to try and put Ashling down for a nap, or else she'll be crabby for Damia later.'

Ajax said, 'Last night—'

She cut him off. 'It was just sex, Ajax. Nothing more. I agree—we need to let this run its course.'

He looked at her for a long moment and then said, 'This conversation isn't over.'

He left the nursery.

Hours later, Ajax waited for Erin in the hall. He felt restless and irritable. She'd managed to successfully avoid him all day—taking Ashling on an excursion to the village, according to Damia.

He would have gone after her, but his mother had waylaid him and said, 'Don't do what we did, Ajax, live half-lives. You deserve more, and you can have that with Erin. I've seen the way she looks at you...'

Ajax still couldn't understand what his mother meant. Erin only ever looked at him warily, or with barely concealed amusement. Like when he'd been exhibiting his pathetic range of culinary skills last night. Culinary skills inspired by her, even though he'd let her go.

Erin's voice came back to him. *'You dumped me.'* He winced. He had dumped her unceremoniously. Because she'd got too close.

'I've seen the way she looks at you.'

Ajax shook his head at himself. His mother was obviously going through some sort of life crisis and was seeing things all over the place.

Erin wanted him at a distance, but she would kill him in the process if last night was anything to go by.

A question formed in his head. If Erin had got too close for comfort before, then where was she now? After all, he'd been prepared to make a lifetime commitment to her. Obviously both being aware that it would be based on companionability and chemistry. Nothing more.

'*You deserve more.*'

But he didn't want more. He didn't want to risk that awful devastation all over again. The loss of someone he—

He heard a sound and turned to see Erin at the top of the stairs. And in that moment—in a heartbeat—he knew that it was all too late.

He'd been fooling himself…living in denial. The one thing he'd promised would never happen again had crept up on him and happened before he could stop it, and he realised now that it had happened even before that second night with Erin.

It was the reason he hadn't slept with anyone else.

It was the reason it had taken him so long to go after her.

Because he'd *known*. Deep down.

Erin looked worried. 'Is the dress okay? It's too short, isn't it? Maybe it's meant to be evening-length, but you did say cocktail.'

Ajax barely took in the dress—it fell to mid-calf and it was strapless and figure-hugging. Not that he needed a reminder of Erin's figure. All he had to do was close his eyes and he was there, under her, as she slid on top of him.

'It's fine. You look amazing… We should go.'

She still looked a bit concerned, but she came down the stairs towards him and panic rose up, making his skin feel tight. He swallowed it down. When Erin got to him her scent tickled his nostrils. Fresh and light. Nothing complicated. Like her. Straight. When what he was feeling right now was anything but straight. It was a maelstrom.

She frowned. 'What is it? You're looking at me like I've done something wrong.'

She had—and she had no idea. She'd upended Ajax's world and it would never be the same again. She'd made a mockery of his notion that he could control everything. That he could protect himself.

But now was not the time or the place to spill his guts.

He lied through his teeth. 'Nothing is wrong. We should go.'

That evening's event was on yet another nearby island— an open-air art exhibition of some of the world's most famous modern artists. All of Ajax's family were there again, but there were other people too, and it was nice to have a sense of the normal world around her. People laughing and chatting.

Erin was delighted to see Leo and Angel Parnassus, and only too happy to let Angel spirit her away from Ajax temporarily. He was in a funny mood. She kept catching him looking at her as if she was someone he didn't know. Suspicious. Accusing.

But if it kept some sort of distance between them then she welcomed it. Because increasingly around him she felt as if she was losing sight of what was important. To keep herself and Ashling safe from harm. From betrayal. From being rejected. Dumped again.

So how does that explain how you gravitated into his bed like a wanton last night?

Erin ignored that and let Angel distract her. She was telling her how this whole social scene was a circuit, which happened every summer for members of Greek's high society, when they decamped from humid Athens to their various island boltholes and then spent a couple of months island-hopping on planes, helicopters or yachts.

It made Erin's mind boggle...the sheer wealth.

Leo and Ajax joined them, and Ajax put an arm around

Erin's waist. She tried to stiffen against the inevitable urge to relax into him, but once again it was easier just to... *cleave*.

Ajax's parents hadn't come with them to this event. Andromeda had actually said that she would help Damia with Ashling. So when they got back to the villa that night it was just them, and a silent villa.

Wordlessly, Erin read Ajax's intent. He took her hand and waited for her to take off her shoes, then led her upstairs to her room. They both went in and checked on Ashling, who was asleep.

Erin was torn between wanting an excuse not to go where they were inevitably headed, and wanting to drag all of Ajax's clothes off him there and then.

He led her out, down to his room. He shut the door behind them and Erin stood with her back to it. He put his hands either side of her head and just looked at her.

Erin said, 'What is it? You've been glaring at me all evening.'

Ajax shook his head. He fingers traced her jaw, his touch gentle, belying the fierceness of his expression.

He said, 'You. You're killing me. I—'

Erin reached up and put her hands on his face, touching her mouth to his, cutting off his words, as if she knew he was going to say something she didn't want to hear.

She broke away after a long moment and said, 'No words. We don't need to talk.'

Ajax was mocking. 'I forgot...this is just sex.'

Erin nodded as she pushed Ajax's jacket off his shoulders to the floor, then tackled his bow tie and shirt. 'Yes, it's just sex.'

For the next couple of hours it *was* just sex—and Erin pushed away every internal voice or twinge of conscience and tried to convince herself of that.

CHAPTER ELEVEN

Two weeks later, Athens

AFTER ERIN HAD cleared a further absence from work—unpaid—it was as if she and Ajax had entered into a tacit agreement to stay in Greece and indulge this desire until it burned out.

At night she would steal into his room, where they would communicate with a primal ferocity that left her breathless and desperate, wondering why their chemistry wasn't waning. The opposite, it felt like.

She was aware of Ajax looking at her more and more as if he wanted to say something, but she would invariably make an excuse to walk away or distract him. Instinctively she knew she didn't want to hear what he might say.

But she felt as if a net was slowly closing around her. She couldn't keep avoiding Ajax for ever. A decision would have to be made. They had to return to New York and get on with their lives. As it was, Erin's firm had been more than generous allowing her all this time off, but she couldn't take advantage for much longer if she expected her job to still be there for her.

And now there was a further potential complication in the mix—one that Erin couldn't even bring herself to fully contemplate. She'd looked at herself in the mirror that morning, after a sudden bout of vomiting, and a feeling of dread coupled with absurd excitement had mixed in her gut—prompting another bout of sickness.

It mightn't be anything, assured an inner voice.

But this was exactly what had happened with Ashling—except she'd ignored it until the point where she hadn't been able to ignore it any longer.

Ashling handed Erin the toy she'd been playing with as they sat under the shade of one of the trees on the lawn in the gardens of Ajax's Athens villa.

'Thank you,' said Erin absently.

And then, as if manifested by her imagination, she looked up and saw Ajax walking across the lawn to them with a determined look on his face. Erin felt like running—and also too weary to run...as if she'd been running for a long time and wanted to stop.

He was dressed in jeans and a shirt—untucked, sleeves rolled up. He'd been working from home today. Ashling saw him and clapped her hands and stood up unsteadily. Ajax crouched down a few feet away and held out his arms, Ashling had no hesitation and ran straight into them, squealing with glee when he lifted her up high into the air, twirling her around.

Erin envied the simplicity of the relationship between them.

Ajax came over and kneeled down, putting Ashling back on the ground, where she pounced on her toys again. He looked at Erin. 'Can we talk?'

Panic flared. A sense of nausea gripped her at the memory of earlier that morning.

'I told Damia I'd help her with an English essay she has due—'

Ajax reached out and caught her hand gently, stopping her from standing.

She stopped and pulled it back.

He said, 'I'd prefer to talk elsewhere, but you keep running away from me every time I try to talk to you.'

'I was in your bed last night,' Erin said, almost accusingly—as if he was responsible for some witchcraft that got her to come to him like some kind of automaton.

Ajax snorted. 'As if that's where we'll get any talking done! Maybe in another ten years, when I don't want you as much as I—'

'We won't be together in ten years.' Erin cut him off, panic rising. The net was closing around her.

'Yes, we will, Erin Murphy. Because I love you, and I've been trying to tell you for days now, and you keep avoiding—'

But she was already on her feet, galvanised by a force deep inside that she couldn't fully understand. All she knew was that she had to leave…get away—*now*.

She started walking blindly up the garden. Ajax called from behind her. 'Dammit, Erin, would you just—? Where are you going?'

She turned around but kept walking backwards. Ajax was holding Ashling in his arms. She was looking confused, putting out her hand. Erin felt emotion rising, threatening to consume her.

'I'm sorry… I can't do this,' she got out, and she fled.

The driver had dropped Erin in the Plaka area of Athens. It was crowded with tourists and locals. She walked blindly for a long time, trying not to think of what Ajax had said.

'I love you.'

He didn't mean it. It was a platitude to get her to agree

to stay with him…to create a life that would fall apart once he lost interest.

Erin recognised a doorway and stumbled to a halt. She went in and was greeted by a doorman, who pressed a button on the elevator for her. She stepped into the dark space, only then recognising it as the restaurant where Ajax had taken her on one of those first nights.

She wanted to turn around and get out, but it was too late. The elevator doors were opening again and a waiter was leading her to a quiet table. There weren't many people. It was between lunch and dinner time. The staff change-over was happening.

A glass of water and a glass of wine materialised in front of her—she didn't even remember ordering them. She took a big gulp of water, but ignored the wine.

'I love you.'

Erin shook her head. But then she thought of Ashling, her face confused, in Ajax's arms, her little hand held out.

A memory rose up, unbidden, of herself as a child, a toddler…crying and pleading, hanging on to her mother's skirt, her hands being prised away, her father lifting her up. And how it had felt to stretch out her hand towards her mother, watching her as she disappeared behind a closed door.

Even at that young age, Erin realised now, she'd believed that somehow *she'd* caused her to leave. Because she'd loved her mother too much and wanted her to stay. So she'd left.

Erin only realised she was crying when she looked up and saw Ajax standing there. He was immediately concerned, coming to her side.

'What is it? Is it really so bad if I love you?'

Erin pushed up out of the chair. She had to get away—

again. She went towards the elevator, barely noticing that the restaurant was now empty.

The doors were open. She got in and stabbed at the buttons—any buttons—to shut the door and push Ajax back.

The doors started closing, but a hand stopped them and Ajax stepped in.

The doors closed. Erin backed away against a wall.

It finally rose up inside her—the truth of what she was feeling. But she couldn't articulate it.

She said, 'Please don't say it again.'

The elevator wasn't moving, but Erin was barely aware.

Ajax said, 'What? That I love you? Well, I do—and I'm going to keep saying it until you believe me.'

Erin shook her head. 'I don't want to believe you. Because if I believe you then you'll destroy me when you walk away. All this time I've been telling myself I'm worried for Ashling, but it's me. I'm scared for me. Because I can't go through it again. Watching my mother walk out broke something inside me.'

Ajax moved to come closer, but Erin put up a hand.

He stopped. 'You're not broken, Erin—far from it. Your mother abandoned you…that's a traumatic event that would scar anyone, let alone a small child.'

'I just walked away from my own daughter.'

Erin felt bile and shame. She'd literally repeated history.

Ajax shook his head. 'You couldn't walk away from your own child and you know it. This is very different.'

Erin's insides cramped. 'Is she okay?'

'She's fine—having dinner with Damia as we speak.'

Erin knew he was right. She would never be able to leave Ashling. She'd walked away from him, from his declaration.

Ajax said, 'It was my fault. I should have waited. But I've

been growing impatient... We've wasted so much time... nearly two years... I want to spend the rest of my life with you, Erin. I want us to have so much more than what we've experienced in our lives.'

She shook her head, emotion rising. She had nothing to hide behind any more. 'I can't love you... I'm too scared of being hurt again.'

Ajax closed the distance between them and this time Erin couldn't stop him. He cupped her face in his hands and looked down at her with an expression she'd never seen before. Or maybe she had, and she'd told herself it wasn't what she thought it was. Feared it was.

Love. The thing she wanted. The thing she feared.

He said, 'It's too late. You already love me. And I love you. I think I've loved you from way back...that second night. That's why I let you go.'

Erin hiccupped. 'You mean dumped me.'

Ajax winced. 'You got too close. I could see myself becoming obsessed. I wasn't ready. But I didn't forget you. And I didn't want anyone else.'

Erin sniffed. 'You're just lucky that I was occupied having your daughter and that someone else didn't sweep me off my feet.'

Ajax went pale in the dim light of the small space. 'Don't even joke about that.'

A tiny, fledgling seed of hope was pushing out of the deep dark fear inside Erin. She said, 'I won't survive if you dump me again.'

Ajax shook his head, and now he looked fierce. 'Losing Theo almost destroyed me. I'd never known love could be like that and I wanted nothing to do with it ever again. But you brought me back to life. And Ashling. You made me want to believe again. To trust again. I'm not going anywhere. And neither are you. We are bound together for ever. I want a family with you. I want to shower our children with all the love and security we missed.'

Erin bit her lip and took Ajax's hand, bringing it to her belly, under her shirt. His eyes widened and she said, 'I don't know for sure, but if my symptoms are anything to go by I could already be pregnant again.'

Ajax's hand spread across Erin's belly. His voice was hoarse. 'Truly?'

She nodded, and felt any last doubts dissolving at the awe on Ajax's face. 'That's why I panicked before and ran. I knew this, and I was afraid that if you didn't really mean what you said…if you were just saying it…then we'd be stuck together unhappily, like your parents and all those other people, for the rest of our lives.'

Ajax shook his head. He entwined his fingers with hers and said, 'Not possible. We're not them and we never will be.'

Then he got down on one knee, and Erin's eyes went wide. He kept her hand in his and said, 'Erin Murphy, will you please marry me, and have a family with me, and love me as I promise to love you, until death us do part?'

Love. The scariest thing of all. But without it she wouldn't survive.

Erin nodded and slid down on to her knees beside him, wrapping her arms around his neck. 'I love you, Ajax.' She was finally home.

Home.

When they emerged from the elevator some time later, a little dishevelled but giddy with happiness, Erin said, 'What is it about us and elevators?'

Ajax said, 'I don't know, but I'm going to make sure there's one in every one of our properties from now on.'

Erin laughed. 'Isn't that a little extravagant?'

Ajax picked up his fiancée, uncaring of who looked at them in the street, and said, 'Well, where else are we going to celebrate our anniversaries?'

'That's very true—but first can we go home to our baby?'

'Now, that...' Ajax kissed her '...we can do.'

EPILOGUE

Three years later

ERIN SMILED AT the scene before her. Chaos, in a word. But very happy chaos.

She was standing on the terrace of the villa in Athens. Where once there had been a pristine empty lawn stretching into the distance, with the majestic city of Athens in the background, now there was a bouncy castle, clowns, too many children to count, adults chatting and warding off minor accidents, tables groaning under the weight of food and drink, and at least two fluffy dogs alternately being pawed at by the children or hiding in the bushes for some respite.

Her father was on one side of the garden, discussing plants with the head gardener. He had a pointed party hat on his head, askew, making him look even more like a mad professor than he usually did.

Then Erin's eyes widened, and she put a hand to her mouth to try and hide a laugh of disbelief. Yes, that really was Ajax's impeccably cool and elegant mother, on the bouncy castle, being thrown hither and thither with any number of children. And she wasn't horrified—she was laughing. Shrieking with delight, in fact. And her sleek cap of grey hair was mussed up in a way that Erin would never have believed possible just a couple of years ago.

Andromeda had changed utterly. She was now a much beloved grandmother, making the most of all the love she'd missed out on with her own children. She'd divorced Ajax's father and since married the man she'd fallen in love with ten years ago. He was watching now from the sidelines, with an indulgent smile.

Erin's mother hadn't had such a radical change of heart, but she was making an effort and she and Erin had found some peace.

Erin had left her job at the firm—understandably, after falling pregnant again—and she'd since decided that she wanted to move into not-for-profit consultancy work. She had set up a firm that helped small businesses who couldn't afford the fees that the big law firms charged. They did a lot of work with charities and marginalised communities. It was unbelievably rewarding, and she loved it.

'*Yaya!* I'm coming!'

Ashling, four years old today, leapt up onto the bouncy castle and promptly upended her grandmother. To say she was fizzing with excitement was an understatement.

Agatha had come from the island to visit, and was currently holding a sleepy toddler in her arms. Teddy. Ajax and Erin had agreed that they would have loved to call him Theo, but it was just too close to the bone. And Theo had been Theo. So they'd settled on Teddy as a compromise. With his dark blond hair showing tints of red, he took after the Murphy side of the family. Except for the light eyes. They were as blue-green as his father's.

The tiny hairs on the back of Erin's neck stood up. She smiled before she even felt him. And then he slid his arms around her distended waist, his hands covering her sizeable bump.

Ajax kissed the side of Erin's neck and her blood hummed. She put her hands over his. No sign of their chemistry waning. It only got stronger.

And soon they would welcome a new member into their family. It was the reason they were here in Athens and not on the island. She was due any day now. Baby number three…

Ajax moved to take her hand and she looked at him. They didn't speak. They didn't need to. They just smiled. The evidence of their love was all around them. It had broken the shackles of the past and brought them here, to this bright and shining place, where love was celebrated daily and where fear was no longer given room to breathe.

He led her down into the garden, and they were soon swallowed up in the joyous, loving mayhem.

* * * * *

*Were you blown away by this Abby Green story?
Then don't miss out on her other
dramatic stories for Presents!*

The Kiss She Claimed from the Greek
A Ring for the Spaniard's Revenge
His Housekeeper's Twin Baby Confession
Mistaken as His Royal Bride
Claimed by the Crown Prince

Available now!